THE MAMMOTH AND THE MOONSTICK

THE
MAMMOTH
AND THE
MOONSTICK

SIMON E WILKINSON

ILLUSTRATED BY CHARLIE TAYLOR

To Angela, Paul and James and my three grandchildren –
Georgia, Jack and Cassie.

In a remote galaxy millions of light years across the universe, another world shimmers like a bright pearl in the star-dappled darkness. Of course no one has ever been there – no one except a young boy who once dared to dream of walking with giants.

This distant planet is identical to ours, except for one thing: there, the ice age has never gone away. Colder than you could ever imagine, where the wild wind whips and chafes, it is permanently covered in a thick crust of ice and snow. Yet in this hostile place the fantastic creatures that disappeared from us a long time ago are still very much alive . . .

IN THE BLEAK MID SUMMER

The large mammoth shivered, lifted her head, and blinked at the darkening sky where heavy grey clouds were squatting unsteadily on the peaks of misty mountains. A thick fog was slowly descending from the upper slopes. She watched it swallowing up the pine trees as it spread its dim shroud over the tundra.

Swirling snow settled on her eyelashes and clung to the thick, brown, matted hair which hung from her body like a straggly wet curtain.

Hoisting her heavy trunk high in the air, she

folded it over her head into a large S shape before opening her mouth to let in the soft, plump, white flakes. They dissolved on her tongue, instantly refreshing her dry mouth.

The deep carpet of snow beneath her feet was being whipped up by a chafing Arctic wind which chanted sad tunes over the great Siberian glacier.

Squinting through the flowing flakes, she watched the snow billow and slither like

white snakes over the icy lake down in the valley. The pale orange sun skated slowly over the horizon. It would be dark soon and the temperature was already falling fast.

The mammoth could feel her baby squirming, kicking, rolling inside her great belly. It was getting ready to be born, but she could not risk bringing her calf into this harsh, frozen world because she knew it would not survive the brutal cold.

Anya stared into the fog; she needed to find a sheltered place where her calf could be born safely, somewhere dry where it could drink her warm milk to give it strength. Without protection from the biting wind, the milk would freeze, and her baby would surely starve.

She knew she had to make her way to Crystal Cave, the special place where all mammoths were born. It would be her refuge from the fierce conditions and even fiercer predators that would try to snatch away her newborn calf.

It was a steep climb up the snowy slopes but she had to reach the cave before it became too dark – or possibly too late.

Lowering her trunk, Anya snorted three times to alert her family who were foraging with their long tusks for fresh grass and plants beneath the snow and ice. When they heard her calling, they lifted their heads and listened. Her two words cut through the wind. 'It's coming!' she cried.

They hurried to her side and quickly decided that Troyka, leader of the herd, would guide Anya to the cave. The others would shelter from the storm among the pine trees and wait for her to return.

The two mammoths set off knowing their journey would be treacherous. They tried to quicken the pace but their progress up the mountain path was terribly slow as they plodded through the thickening snow.

CALL OF THE WILD

Six kilometres to the west a black nose twitched and sniffed at familiar smells borne on the stiff, cold wind. It was a scent that Kirill the alpha wolf recognised. He knew well the earthy, musty aroma of mammoth and that meant only one thing to him – food.

Kirill sucked fresh air into his lungs and raised his head to the sky.

'Whooooohhh!' With this triumphant howl, he called the wolf pack to his side. But they had already picked up the scent. Licking their lips and whimpering obedience to their leader, they gathered around Kirill to join him in a frenzy of howling,

' W h o o o o o o W o o o o o h h h
W h o o o w o o o o w o o o h h h !
W h o o o o o W o o o o o o o o o o o o h h ! '

Their high-pitched calls trembled through the night air. Restless reindeer and bison raised their heads fearfully as they listened to the wild wolfish shrieks. Taunted by the eerie sound, and having no idea how near or far away the wolf dogs were, they scampered for cover among the thick pine trees.

The wolf-cries stretched out far and wide in the dusk of early evening, their deathly warning tripped over the tundra, echoing between the snow-clad mountains.

Buffeted by strong winds, and amplified by rocky cliffs, the eerie calls skated out across the wide, frozen lake. They slid over stiff waterfalls making long slender icicles vibrate and moan tunelessly like a quivering choir of opaque ghosts.

High in the Siberian mountains a sabre-toothed tiger heard the wolf calls and gathered her two cubs to her side. Saiba hadn't eaten for several days. Hunger chewed at her insides; her cubs were restless for food but she had nothing to give them. Her dry lips peeled slowly back over the two long fangs which jutted like scimitars from her scowling cruel mouth.

As she listened to the distant howls, Saiba's hunger pangs turned to fear. She knew that a lone wolf would be no match for her fierce fighting skills, but a whole wolf pack? Well that was a different matter completely. Although her whimpering cubs were slowly starving, they would have to wait a while longer before they could eat.

'Quickly come with me little ones,' she whispered

to them. Silently, reluctantly, they retreated deep into their mountain lair.

Muffled by the thick foliage of pine trees, the wolves' howls fell silent in the forests that skirted the lower hills. Peering through the thickening snowflakes the remaining mammoths watched Troyka and Anya follow the long narrow trail to Crystal Cave, until they were swallowed up by the fog sprouting like a thick beard on the face of the mountain.

Berta strained her eyes. 'Can anyone still see them?' she whispered.

Winnie shook her head. 'No, but I am sure they will be fine,' she told her firmly. But truthfully, she wasn't sure at all.

After watching them disappear, the family, led by Berta, retreated into the calm shelter of the trees.

Kirill raised his nose into the wind. By now he had picked up the fresh scent of the two large mammoths that had peeled away from the rest of the herd. Instantly, he guessed they were heading for the cave inside Crystal Mountain. It was a place he knew well for he had been there before; it was where he had first tasted a mammoth. He licked his lips at the memory of the juicy, bitter-sweet tastes. 'Quick, follow me!' he panted. The wolves turned eastwards in the direction of the fabled Crystal Cave with its sparkling glass walls.

Far above the clouds, where the pack had bayed at the moon, the piercing calls of the wailing wolves continued to climb upwards through the sky before arrowing across the breathless universe toward glistening stars in unknown galaxies. But by the time their proud shrieks finally settled on distant planets and dusty moons, the dogs' war cries had shrivelled to little more than faint whispers – so no one heard them. No one, except a young boy called Tom Lennox who was just about to fall asleep when the last few drops of the wolfish howls tumbled onto the soft pillow next to his ear.

'Whooooohhh ... Whooooohhh ...'

HOWLING OLD OWL?

It was eleven o'clock on a warm summer night; Tom had been trying to get to sleep, but the more he concentrated on getting there, the further it slipped away from him. And through his open bedroom window came disturbing sounds from the garden.

'Wooit wooit toohooo,' came the hoot of a bored tawny owl perched in a nearby tree.

'Yeah "Wooit wooit toohooo" to you too!' groaned Tom in mock imitation.

'Wooit wooit toohooo!' replied the owl more

woorit wooit toohoo... perkily, believing it had found a mate somewhere in the darkness. 'Pleeeeaaasse go away!' shrieked Tom.

The owl fanned its wingtips and silently obliged. Everything went quiet.

'Thank goodness for that,' murmured Tom. But just as he was settling on a dream, he heard the faint unfamiliar calls of the wolves, 'Whooooohhh… Whooooohhh…' He began puzzling over what had made the noise. A dog barking? No not a dog. _Perhaps It had been a badger then? No_, he decided, _it wasn't a badger either._ But what could it have been?

He was mystified. It had sounded somehow softer, somehow sadder, like a howl from a distant fox. But that wasn't a fox at all, he was sure of that. Maybe it had been the owl again. *No, this was more of a Whooooohhh than a Wooit wooit toohooo – there was a difference,* he decided with a frown: *owls hoot; they don't howl.* And so, with the word *howl* whirling in his mind, Tom Lennox fell fast asleep.

LONG TREK UP THE MOUNTAIN

Anya's family were sheltering among the trees, munching on pine cones and snuffling under the snow for juicy grass stalks. Tilting their heads and straining their ears, they listened to the wolves' ghoulish moans riding the swift wind between the mountains.

'Any idea how close the wolves are?' asked Berta with a quivering voice. The mammoths shook their heads. 'Do you think Anya and Troyka will be okay? They're out there on the bare mountain,' she added nervously. 'Maybe we should go out there to be with them.'

'No! Anya wouldn't want us to do that,' said Truba firmly. 'That would put us all in danger. We must stay here and wait for Troyka to come back.'

As feelings of fear and gloom gathered around them, the mammoths huddled together listening intently to the wolves' pitiful shanties.

Then the howling ceased abruptly. It was followed by an eerie silence . . . Bad news! A warning to all creatures that the cruel pack was now on the move and on the hunt.

The pale moon continued to probe gaps between the clouds and fog as it guided Anya and Troyka with its weak light toward Crystal Cave. Slowly, with their heads bowed, they trudged through the blizzard.

As they climbed higher into the mountain, wild winds howled like banshees, diluting the dense fog to a thin ghostly mist.

Even though they both knew the area well, familiar landmarks rapidly dissolved in the swirling snow. The mammoths, confused by the changing landscape, had lost their sense of direction and were starting to lose hope of ever finding the cave.

The temperature dipped further and they both began to shiver with the cold and also the fear of knowing that the wolves were out there – somewhere.

Anya, heavy with her unborn calf, struggled in the deepening snow. Her legs were weakening; twice after crumpling to the frozen ground, she felt Troyka's long tusks slip through the snow beneath her body to gently hoist her back onto her feet. They ploughed on through the blizzard. When they arrived at a flat plateau, Troyka bellowed a snort of delight. He straightened his great trunk and pointed to a low hill.

'Look over there,' he whispered. They had found

what they were looking for. Through narrowed eyes, Anya recognised the familiar shape of the large round stone guarding the cave. Icicles dangled like broken teeth over its mouth. Snow was drifting at the entrance. They had arrived just in time.

Thicker, heavier black clouds sailed silently overhead switching off the moon's pale light. The mountain was swallowed up in an eerie darkness. Large flakes of snow cascaded all around Troyka and Anya as the swirling wind probed and parted their thick fur.

The terrible storm was far worse than Troyka could ever remember. He peered into the gloom and blinked as a shaft of fluorescent lightning wriggled out from a distant cloud, setting the sky on fire for a few precious moments. It lit up the valley with a warning of even more severe weather to come.

Troyka could see that a dark storm was brewing like a thick black soup in the heavens. The wise mammoth knew that very soon, everywhere would be engulfed in deep snowdrifts.

He needed to act quickly. With room for only one mammoth inside the cave, Troyka pushed aside the great boulder with ease and ushered Anya inside. He needed to make sure she was safe before he could descend to the lower slopes and rejoin his family.

Anya had become exhausted by the long, steep climb to reach the cave. She needed to rest. Troyka felt sad because he didn't want to leave her all alone, but what choice did he have? Lovingly, he brushed her soft cheek with his trunk and promised to come back in a few days.

'You'll be fine,' he told her calmly. 'The cave's mystic crystals will protect you.'

Anya trusted Troyka – she believed in the magic power of the crystal walls that lined the cave.

Once she was safely in, Troyka pushed his powerful shoulder against the huge round stone. It rolled over the icy ground, snapping away the shimmering icicles, before forming a perfect seal across the entrance.

SET IN STONE

Anya was finally alone in the darkness. Using her trunk to feel her way around, she probed the chilly, damp walls. Her strong ivory tusks clattered against the cold crystal as she blindly searched for a dry patch in the murky cave where she could bring her calf into the world. Her sensitive ears picked out occasional drips of water and the sound of small creatures scurrying about. She found a comfortable patch of ground where she lay down and waited patiently for her calf to come.

After sealing Anya inside the cave, Troyka set off to rejoin the other mammoths. The swirling gusts of wind grew stronger, forcing him back, as he made his way cautiously down the mountain path.

Thick fog was waiting on the lower slope to wrap itself around him. It seemed to cling to his face and body as he bravely stepped into it, feeling his way with his trunk to retrace the footsteps they had made earlier.

Troyka knew he could do no more for Anya. He was satisfied that he had helped her as much as he could. At least she was safe and secure.

But was Anya really safe? Twelve dark shadows were silently stealing through the night. When the wolves arrived at the entrance to Crystal Cave they wagged their tails excitedly and sniffed at the edges of the giant boulder.

Their keen sense of smell told them that a large beast lurked inside. But Kirill knew more than that;

he turned and sneered at his simpering pack. He brushed his long purple tongue between his teeth and lips as he relished the sweet taste of fresh food. And if Kirill's instinct was right, there would be a special bonus for his faithful followers, because his glistening nose, which never lied, told him that the single mammoth inside the cave had just become two: a little calf had been born.

The grovelling wolves crawled alongside Kirill. They pawed and scratched at the entrance but there was no way past the large rock which had been wedged there by Troyka.

Kirill was a wise old wolf; he knew they needed to be patient. 'Wait!' he whispered. 'The mammoth must come out soon and when she does, we will attack.'

He barked a stern command to the pack to lie down. Obediently, they dug beds into the wet snow to shelter from the growing storm.

Troyka finally made it to the lower valley and rejoined his family sheltering among trees. There was little any of them could do for now except hope that the terrible blizzard would soon blow over. They would have to wait and see the storm out before they could even think about rescuing Anya.

PREPARING FOR TAKE-OFF

It was exactly 3:27am when Tom Lennox sat upright in his bed.

'Wolves!' he screamed. He was certain that was what the sound had been!

His voice echoed through the slumbering household. In the next room his sister Katie stirred in her sleep. Her eyes flickered briefly but, overcome with tiredness, she was soon back among her dreams. Their father continued to snore peacefully, greeting Tom's cry with little more than a fleeting grunt.

Tom was too excited for sleep. He lay back, cradling his head in his open hands. *But there are no wolves – except for the zoo, and that's a long way from here,* he thought. *Was their calling some kind of invitation to another exciting adventure?*

Breathlessly, he opened his bedside drawer and took out the incredible gift handed to him by a weird woman called Susan Dior at the museum. It was a shoe box stuffed with tiny wooden dinosaurs and a virtual reality headset. She had included a note which Tom had read many times over. He scanned it once more:

Hello Tom, I hope you have lots of exciting prehistoric adventures. Let your imagination take you back in time. Hold one of the little figures in your hand, stroke it with your fingers, then put on the magic goggles – an incredible world will open up before you.

Susan Dior.

Tom was puzzled. There were no wolves in the box – he knew perfectly well that dinosaurs had died out a long time before any wolves lived on earth. So why had he heard their cries?

He considered it for a while before finally closing the lid. *I must be wrong,* he thought, *maybe I just dreamt it.* But as he was replacing the box, a small wooden figure lurking at the back of the drawer caught his eye.

He plucked it out and examined it carefully. It wasn't a dinosaur at all; it was a perfectly carved woolly mammoth which had definitely not been in the gift pack Susan had given him.

'Now where did you come from?' Tom muttered.

As his hands gently stroked the baby mammoth, he felt a surge like a tiny electric current fizzing through his fingers and up into his arms. It was the same familiar sensation that had whisked him away on so many exciting dinosaur adventures.

Now he felt sure that he was going on a journey back through time and space, and if his guess was right, he wouldn't be seeing any dinosaurs at all. Instead, his adventure would take him to a much colder place to meet the majestic mammoths that had once roamed the earth.

Excitedly, he clutched the little figure knowing all he needed to spark the magic of time-travel was the special 3D headset. He reached out and took it from the box. Tom was impatient; he wanted his journey to begin right away. He was about to slip the goggles over his eyes but stopped as soon as his fingers explored the tiny rough figure in more detail. A thought came into his head. Although Tom didn't know too much about mammoths, he knew they had been called woolly for a very good reason. These beasts were covered in dense fur which helped them survive the coldest climate on earth – the Ice Age.

Tom shivered at the thought. So far, on his travels he had only ever faced the hot Jurassic sun. But this would be different. Much of the world was covered in large glaciers during the Pleistocene period. He was going to need something much thicker than a thin nylon anorak and wellington boots to keep out the cold. But what? He didn't have anything else, certainly nothing suitable. Hmmm, but he knew someone who did . . .

Sneaking into his sister's bedroom Tom switched on her small bedside lamp. Katie never murmured: she was fast asleep.

Inside her wardrobe he found a number of items that would come in handy for an Arctic adventure. Her fur-lined boots should keep out the cold, as would her heavy cream duffel coat. After a further search he unfolded Katie's favourite winter jumper emblazoned with the face of a smiling woolly mammoth adorned by flecks of snow. *How very appropriate,* thought Tom. *Now what else? I'll need some gloves;* he found a pair on a shelf. He would borrow them all and put everything back before morning – she wouldn't even know they'd been taken. Besides, it was August so his sister wouldn't need these items for several months. Finally, he grabbed a scarf for his voyage; he picked

out the longest, woolliest one he could find. Pink and purple! *– Yuk! Not good for camouflage,* he thought, *but I could hide it inside my coat. It will have to do.*

Switching off Katie's lamp, Tom returned to his room and pulled on the thick jumper, gloves and her heavy woollen coat. After stepping into her sheepskin-lined boots he felt prepared for his adventure. Then he caught sight of himself in the mirror. *It's a good thing my friends can't see me now*, he pondered. *But who cares? At least I will be warm and dry.*

Just to be sure of keeping warm, he stuffed a knitted blanket together with Katie's scarf into his backpack and finally, after adding a small solar-powered torch to his luggage, he was ready for his adventure.

Taking a deep breath, he slipped the special goggles over his face and tightened the strap until they fitted snugly. As he caressed the little mammoth, Tom felt the familiar tingle of electricity pulsing through his fingers. His fantastic journey was beginning. Surging far above the clouds, he was soon staring into infinite darkness. Distant stars seemed to be accelerating towards him. Over his shoulder he could see blue planet Earth rapidly shrinking as he jolted further and further into deep space.

He didn't know it, but he was retracing the route that had earlier brought the eerie sound of the wolves to his bedroom. He was moving at an incredible speed, zipping past comets and meteors with ease.

Slipping between the bright stars of Ursa Minor, Tom turned right and shot through the inky blackness before plunging into a cosmic spiralling black hole which spat him out into distant, uncharted reaches of the universe. He marvelled at blurry planets and stars as he whirred past them.

In the distance he spotted a single white globe shivering in a far corner of this unknown galaxy. A planet wrapped in a thick blanket of fog, snow and ice; ancient Earth welcomed him with a shudder.

BEAST FROM THE EAST

When he finally arrived, Tom had expected to be greeted by the very worst of winter weather. He had imagined cruel relentless winds, frozen plains and snowy mountain peaks; a total whiteout stretching as far as the eye could see.

Slipping the rucksack from his back he took off his goggles and put them away as he waited for his eyes to adjust to the light. But there was no light – only darkness. Tom had once read that for several months of the year, Arctic regions were plunged into permanent night time. Was this happening now? He looked above. Why were there no stars in the sky? he wondered. Why no wind, nor any snow?

He decided to do some exploring but needed to illuminate his way. Delving into his backpack, he spilled all the contents on the damp ground as he rummaged for his torch. As he stooped and fumbled to pick them up, he heard the muffled sound of shallow breathing.

'Hello! Hello! Who's there?' he whispered. The only reply was a vague echo of his own voice. Tom realised that he must be inside some sort of cavern. He listened for more sounds in the spooky silence.

'I know you're there,' Tom chattered nervously. He sensed an animal close by – he could smell it, but he had no idea what it was, or if his life was in danger.

He switched on his torch, instantly flooding the cave with dazzling light. He was in a room filled with mirrors. Shadows danced menacingly like grey phantoms as his beam picked out transparent columns of rock. The splintering shafts of light bounced off walls gleaming like polished silver.

Suddenly, a giant loomed angrily from the cold shadows, thrusting its spear-like tusks towards him.

Tom stared open-mouthed at the mammoth. She was simply huge – much bulkier and taller than any elephants he had ever seen. Her two curved tusks were easily four metres in length, twice that of an elephant's, and one of them was perilously close to his face.

Smelly breath-clouds erupted from her mouth, coating Tom's face and clothes with the sweet sickly aroma of fermented grass. As he lurched back in surprise, his torchlight landed on a small bundle of fur nestling near the giant's feet. Looking exactly like the carved figure in his bedside drawer, it was the

young mammoth he had been hoping to find.

Its angry mother moved swiftly to defend her calf from this stranger. She pinned Tom against a cold clammy wall. He was unable to move.

'No, stop!' he cried. 'I am not here to hurt you – or your calf. My name is Tom Lennox, I—'

'Well if you're not here to harm us, why are you here at all, and how did you sneak into this cave?' She eyed Tom suspiciously.

The mammoth pressed him even harder with a single tusk. She stretched out her long trunk and sniffed at his thick white coat.

'What are you – a snow bear?' she shrieked. Tom swallowed hard, shaking his head.

'You are . . . aren't you? You're a young polar bear! Yes, that's exactly what you are. Where are your parents?' she asked nervously.

Even though the mammoth's tusk was now

digging into his ribs, Tom tried to remain calm. He could see she was determined to protect her baby. And he knew that if she really wanted to hurt him, she would have done it by now.

'No, no, you are wrong! I'm not a bear at all,' he said, fumbling at the toggles of his coat.

'Well you look a bit like a bear, but I have to admit that if you are one, you are very peculiar.'

'I've already told you, I'm not a bear,' he persisted. 'Look, have you ever seen any bear do this?'

Nervously untoggling his coat, Tom showed her the mammoth emblazoned on his sister's jumper. She was amazed.

'Wow! Is that supposed to be me?'

'It could be if you had a smile on your face instead of a scowl,' he replied cheekily.

Anya's mood lightened and she grinned at him.

'You are right, I've never seen a bear do that,' she

glanced at his jumper. They eyed each other through the yellow beam of light.

'Okay, I give in, but you do look a bit like one. So I'm going to call you erm, Little Bear ... by the way, my name is Anya.'

'But I'm not a bear, Anya, I'm a boy,' he said tenderly. 'And would you mind taking your tusk away? You're hurting me!'

Anya stepped back to examine him. 'A boy? You mean you're a human?'

Tom nodded. But instantly he saw that the mammoth had become wary of him once more.

With a steely glare, she leant forward and pressed him back against the wall. 'Humans are our enemy!' she growled. 'You are even more cruel and murderous than a pack of hungry wolves.' She told Tom she had heard about tribes of men armed with spears trapping and killing mammoths and other animals.

'Are you capable of doing that to me and my little calf, Tom? Is that what you are planning to do?'

Tom shook his head vigorously. 'Nnno, no Anya. Never!'

But she wasn't convinced: she needed to be certain her baby was safe. Once again, the mammoth raised her tusks to threaten him.

Tom realised his life was in danger; he could tell she didn't know whether to trust him.

'Please don't worry,' he said soothingly. 'We humans are not all like that, I'm certainly not, and I haven't come here to hurt you, or your calf.' These words seemed to calm Anya; once again she removed her tusk from his chest and stepped back.

'So where have you come from? How did you sneak in here?'

Tom tried to explain how he had travelled from a time and place far in the future but when he finished telling her his incredible story she looked even more doubtful.

'Have you ever had adventures with mammoths before?' she asked.

'Well, no,' said Tom, remembering his tussles with tyrannosaurs. 'I've travelled much further back in time, but I've never seen a mammoth before.'

Anya screwed her eyes in disbelief. 'Rubbish! What nonsense!'

'If it helps you to believe me, I have met some wonderful dinosaurs,' he told her. 'But you'd only think I was making it all up if I told you about them.'

'Dinosaurs… what are they?'

'Erm,' Tom stroked his chin. 'Well, they are sort of giant lizards—'

'Lizards? I've never heard of a lizard – giant or otherwise,' she snorted. 'Don't bother trying to explain any more, I don't believe such a fanciful story for a minute!' she told him harshly. 'Anyway you don't scare me – even if you are a human. Look at you, you're far too small to do me any harm!'

'Well I'm glad to hear you say that Anya, because I don't want to scare you. In fact I would like us to be friends.'

'Friends? Huh I don't know about that!' she spluttered. 'I think that's a step too far, I don't even know if I can truly trust you. But I suppose I have no choice because right now our lives are in terrible danger.'

PLAN OF ESCAPE

Tom looked startled. 'We are in danger? How come?'

'There's a pack of starving wolves outside who would love to get their teeth into a juicy mammoth like me. I'm sure they like humans just as much,' she eyed him up and down. 'Even though you are a bit scrawny!' she added sarcastically. 'But for now there's no way they can get in here because the entrance is sealed up.'

'Sealed up? Then that'll be the reason this place

is so dark,' said Tom, as he flashed his torchlight around the walls and ceiling of the cold cavern.

'Yes, and because it's night time …Durrrr!' she said mockingly.

'Well there's no need for sarcasm,' Tom scolded. Then he held up his hand as a thought crossed his mind. 'Hold on Anya, if we're sealed in here, it means the three of us are trapped.'

She nodded knowingly. 'I'm afraid you're right Little Bear. There's no way of escape, as far as I know there is only one entrance to Crystal Cave and it's covered by a giant boulder.'

'Crystal Cave, is that what this place is called?' Anya nodded. 'So how did you manage to get in here if it's all sealed up?' he asked.

She told him how Troyka had rolled the huge stone across the entrance when he left her all alone.

'Can't you just push it away yourself?' he asked.

'You look big and powerful enough.'

Anya shook her head ruefully.

'Well, maybe we could move it if we pushed hard together,' suggested Tom.

'If you think I'm powerful, you should meet Troyka! He's much stronger than both of us put together . . . in any case, why would we want to move the stone? It's keeping us safe right now.'

Tom thought for a moment. 'Hmmm. Well perhaps we could distract the wolves somehow then make a run for it.'

Anya laughed scornfully. 'Make a run for it? You must be joking! No chance! My little calf is only just strong enough to walk, she can't run yet. In any case you could never outrun a wolf Tom, not even the reindeer can do that. Wolves never give up the chase; they just keep coming after you until you are exhausted. They hunt you down,' she shrugged, 'It's what they do.'

Tom frowned pensively. 'Yeah but if we can somehow get to your family, we might all be safe.'

Anya shook her head briskly. 'No, we'd never get away. I have heard the wolves whimpering and scratching at the stone. They are camped outside this cave waiting for me to make a move. There's no way we can get past them.'

Tom put the tips of his fingers to his lips in deep thought. 'Hmmm, well they don't know I'm here do they? Are you sure there isn't another way out?' he asked.

'Well, no mammoth has ever ventured deep into the back of this cave Tom, we can't squeeze through little holes or tight spaces like you might be able to do. So you see, your scrawniness might turn out to be a good thing after all!'

Ignoring the remark Tom thought for a while longer. 'Okay, I have a plan; I'm going to do some exploring. So you just sit tight and look after your baby. If I find a way, I'll sneak out and bring Troyka back here to rescue you.'

Anya seemed unconvinced. 'You mean you'll vanish and I won't ever see you again!'

'No, not at all!' Tom said firmly. 'You are going to have to trust me Anya,' he paused for a moment. 'Look if it makes you feel any better, I'll bring all your family here. They'll want to see the new member of the herd,' he nodded towards the calf. 'Surely the wolves wouldn't attack a full herd of mammoths . . . would they?'

She shrugged. 'They might, if they were hungry enough. They would force us to separate, pick out a straggler and then they move in for the kill.'

'Okay, so where will I find your family and how many are there?'

'There are four,' she reeled off their names, 'I've already mentioned our leader Troyka, then there's

Truba, you'll easily recognise him because he has a huge flared trunk, and finally we have Winifred and Berta who were born at the same time from the same mother . . . do you know how rare that is in the mammoth world?'

'So they're twins?'

Anya scrunched her eyes together in confusion. 'No, obviously not! They are mammoths – just like me.'

'Yes, I realise that, but if they were born together they must be twins – that's what we call them.'

'Well, I've never heard that word before . . . twins,' she repeated. 'Hmmm I think I like that word. Anyway, until recently, even we couldn't tell them apart because they both looked exactly the same as each other. But that changed when Winnie had a little accident and half of her tusk snapped off.'

'Ouch!' grimaced Tom.

'Yeah exactly. Oh, before I forget: when you

bump into Truba, I don't expect you'll get any sense out of him ... he can be a bit dim sometimes, but he's lovely really. We call him our gentle giant. You are better off talking to Troyka; he will know what needs to be done to get us out of this cave.'

Anya gave him directions to the forest down in the valley. 'If you find a way out of the cave, you'll need to keep out of sight. Please be careful, Little Bear, those wolves are very dangerous but caves are treacherous too. Don't get stuck. Oh, and watch out for any falling rocks!'

'Yes mum,' he grinned.

Anya stuck out her tongue, 'Now who's being sarcastic?'

'Well you are a mum,' said Tom, letting the beam from his torch fall like a spotlight on the sleeping calf. 'Is it a he or a she?'

'"It!"' she replied huffily, 'is female. As you can

see, she has no tusks. Don't you know anything about mammoths? When males are born their tiny tusks are already starting to show; hers will take a little longer to come through.'

'Really? I didn't know that.' He silently wondered whether anyone else in his world knew this strange fact about baby mammoths. 'Probably not,' he blurted.

'Pardon?'

'Sorry, Anya, I was just thinking about something. I didn't mean to say "probably not" out loud.'

'So, how many baby mammoths have you actually come across Tom?'

'Erm, now let me think . . .' Tom started counting on his fingers but she could tell he was teasing.

'None!' screamed Anya in mock annoyance. 'You've never seen one before have you?'

'Nope, none at all.' Tom put his fingers away and looked sheepishly at the floor. 'In fact I've never seen any mammoth before,' then remembering the skeleton he had seen at the Natural History Museum in London, he added, 'at least not a real-life one.'

The temperature seemed to be dropping; Tom noticed the little calf shivering and shuddering on the cold ground. He pulled the knitted blanket from his backpack and unselfishly draped it over her.

The cave fell silent as Anya thought long and hard about what Tom had just told her. She seemed confused.

'So you say you have never seen a mammoth before?'

'Never,' he repeated.

'I don't understand,' she said. 'Aren't there any where you come from?'

Tom shook his head.

'How come?' she asked. 'And if that's true how could you know what we look like?' She pointed her trunk at the mammoth emblazoned on his jumper.

'It's a long story Anya, I'm sorry to say there isn't very much ice left where I come from. In fact before too long there may be none at all,' he added solemnly.

'So where will all the ice creatures live if that happens?' she asked.

'Hopefully, it won't come to that; maybe we'll all come to our senses and save their environment.' They stared gloomily at each other.

WHAT'S IN A NAME?

'Hey, Anya, I've just had a thought.'

The mammoth put her head to one side, 'Okay tell me what it is.'

'Well, you don't have a name for your little calf yet, and I was just thinking if she had been a male, you could have called him Tom . . . after me,' he joked.

'Now why would I want to do that?' Anya replied with a grimace.

'I don't know, maybe something to remember me

by after I've gone home? It was just a thought, that's all.'

'Well she's not a male, so I won't,' she told him decisively. 'In any case, if I had wanted to name her after you, I would call her Little Bear!'

As he turned away to explore the cave, she called out to him. 'Hey, where did you get your moonstick?'

'Moonstick? What moonstick?' he shot her a puzzled look.

She nodded at the object he was holding. 'That thing you're carrying. How does it bring moonlight inside this dark place? It's magical!'

'Oh you mean this?'

Tom flashed his torch around the cavern, dazzling Anya with its brilliant light. The crystal walls and ceiling gleamed like smooth polished silver in the reflected glare filling her eyes with wonder.

She had heard about the magical, protective power of the cave but she had never seen the beautiful, shiny gemstones sparkle with so much splendour.

From the tall uneven ceiling, sharp swords hung in neat rows. Were they shimmering crystal stalactites or slender icicles? Tom wasn't sure, but he decided that if he couldn't find a way out of the cave, he might be able to snap one off and use it to fend off the wolves.

He held out his torch for her to take a closer look. 'You're right Anya, it is magical, because it steals light from the moon to help me see in the dark,' he fibbed. 'It's called a torch, but I think I prefer your name for it, so from now on, it will be my moonstick.' Then with a broad smile, he winked and disappeared deep into the cave.

Anya lay down with her calf and waited. She watched his flickering light fade into the darkness; she heard his footsteps growing fainter, then he was gone.

After several minutes, when Tom hadn't returned,

she began to worry that he might be stuck in a tiny tunnel where she wouldn't be able to help him.

TOM LENNOX WOZ 'ERE

Tom entered a second chamber studded with flashing stalactites looking like crystal chandeliers twinkling and sparkling majestically in his bright light. But as he gazed around, he gasped with surprise because someone had been here before. Humans!

The glassy walls were covered with drawings and etchings of animals – mostly mammoths, but wolves, oxen, and reindeer also lay at the feet of jeering hunters.

As he looked closer, Tom found more pictures of stricken animals; next to them stood matchstick men, some with their arms raised, others jabbing, thrusting, and attacking their prey with arrows, spears and axes.

His mind was racing. *Where were these ancient men now? Had they abandoned the cave?* On the floor he found the charred remains of fires that had burnt out long ago. Scraps of scorched wood mingled with piles of ash and discarded bones and antlers.

He imagined a tribe of primitive men and women, and of boys and girls wrapped in animal skins huddled around the flames, grunting, chewing meat, gnawing on the bones that were now strewn across the floor of the cave. He briefly wondered how they lived and

68

how they coped with the freezing temperatures.

He stepped forward and carefully examined the drawings. One showed hunters trapping and killing two wolves. In another picture, two mammoths had been slain; the poor animals were lying on the ground surrounded by dancing men brandishing their weapons.

He gaped at the carnage. This was exactly what Anya had described. 'No wonder she had been unwilling to trust me,' he murmured quietly to himself.

As his whisper echoed eerily around the chamber, Tom decided to press on by following a route marked out by a series of strange shapes gouged into the wall. They seemed to lead the way until they disappeared beside a dark hole. It was another passage.

Brighter thoughts entered Tom's head – had these prehistoric people known of another way out?

A possible escape route in case they were invaded by wild animals or other tribes. Maybe it's a shortcut up through the mountain.

As he stepped forward, he felt something pressing into the sole of his boot. He picked it up to take a closer look. It was an oval chunk of crystal, slightly larger than a hen's egg, that fitted snugly into the palm of his hand. One of its edges had been sharpened into a crude blade that had become worn and scratched. Tom realised the rock he was holding had been used by ancient hands to engrave the cruel cave pictures.

Returning to the wall art, he raised the small crystal stone and hurriedly etched an extra drawing to the mural before adding his initials – T.L.

He sniggered at the thought that one day someone might discover the Stone Age drawings and ponder over the mysteriously modern image that had been added.

Disappearing into the dark hole, he began climbing sharply up through a damp, narrow tunnel, its walls gleaming in the yellow light.

'Tom! Tom are you there? Can you hear me? Are you okay?' Several times Anya called out his name but there was no reply. She thought about what he had told her and started to suspect that his story about time travel and giant lizards – disonores or dirosauns or whatever he called them – had all been fibs. She wondered if he had already vanished as mysteriously as he had arrived.

Anya's voice drifted from the cave. 'Tom can you hear me? Are you okay?'

Outside, the wolves heard the mammoth's muffled cries. They began to stir with excitement, their ears stiffening as they listened.

Kirill lifted his head. 'Oh yes we can hear you alright,' he muttered. 'So,' he whispered to his pack, 'the mammoth has had her baby. Did you hear her calling to it just now? It sounded like she shouted "Tom". That must be the name she's given it.' He licked his nose with satisfaction. Now it was just a matter of waiting; soon they would be tucking into a mammoth-size feast.

AN UNLIKELY GUARDIAN ANGEL

Tom could hear the spooky echo of Anya's faint calls as he scrambled deeper and deeper into the mountain over loose shale.

There were other sounds too: the faint clicking of tiny feet and claws as small beetles and rats zigzagged across his path. He could make out long tails slipping through tiny cracks in the walls. He let out a muffled squeal whenever he felt a rat scrabbling over his boots as it scampered away.

But there was one special rat that didn't disappear

from view.

As he neared the end of the corridor, he could see there were no more tunnels to the right; there was nothing to his left either. He had come to a dead-end. The torchbeam caught the reflection of razor-sharp teeth and the steely glare of wild, beady eyes staring at him through the gloom. Tom's shoulders slumped with disappointment.

Unlike the other fearful rodents that scampered away, a large grey rat sat on its haunches preening itself as it watched Tom hauling himself along the floor.

Rather than showing any fear, it almost seemed to be smiling and signalling as if beckoning him to the end of the tunnel.

He realised it could be leading him into a trap. *Maybe it has nowhere to run,* he thought.

'Oh, no you don't!' muttered Tom. 'I'm not falling for that trick.' People had told him stories about how rats can become savage when cornered. He was about to turn around in the tunnel, when it suddenly gave out a piercing shriek.

Once again, its eyes blazed brightly. Oddly, Tom felt sure it was trying to tell him something. The rat unexpectedly leapt up and vanished into an overhead space that Tom had failed to notice.

He crawled cautiously to the spot where the rodent had disappeared and looked up. It was a vertical shaft, about 20 metres high, pitted with hand-holds and jutting crystal rocks that made climbing easy.

Tom had expected the grinning rat to be waiting when he reached the top of the shaft, but there was no sign of it. He pressed on. Deeper into the mountain, his route followed a steep upward slope which curved away into blackness.

The light from his moonstick sparkled and glinted on the crystal quartz. Seeping water oozed like sweat from deep cracks in the glossy walls that were closing in around him. The jagged ceiling was now only centimetres above his head and it began to descend rapidly until eventually, he was forced to crawl on his hands and knees. Now he was down among the giant beetles that fed on the rat droppings. The thought made his spine tingle; he was starting to feel queasy and more than a little scared.

Many times he considered giving up but he knew he couldn't let Anya down, so he carried on through the cold, wet passages, grimacing whenever he felt creatures trampolining onto his back before scuttling away. Tom tried to shout back down the tunnels to let Anya know he was alright but his voice had become no more than a stifled gargle in the stale, cold, moist air.

Peering ahead, he could see the passage disappearing among the shadows. He came to a sharp turn and crawled over a pile of fallen rocks.

Tom felt sure he would soon arrive at a dead-end.

He didn't see the sharp, jutting crystal which gashed his forehead. A tiny trickle of blood made its way down his cheek and dripped from his chin. He felt sad and dejected.

Perhaps Anya was right, maybe there was only one way out of this place and the wolves had it covered. He pushed on through a tapering tunnel and when it became too narrow, he slipped off his rucksack, looped the strap over his leg, and slid on his belly, dragging the backpack behind him.

BREAKTHROUGH

Deeper and deeper he crawled inside the mountain. By now he was finding it hard to breathe because the still air was so stale. His heart was beating quickly as he fought to suck oxygen out of the thin atmosphere. Although the light from his moonstick easily penetrated the darkness, he could hardly see anything for the clouds of breath bubbling like scalding steam from his mouth and nose.

As he made his way along the dingy passage, the only sound Tom could hear was the tip, tip, tapping of a scurrying rat or beetle.

Once again, he thought of abandoning his search. He was fairly sure by now that there was no other way out of the cave. Hauling himself painfully over fallen stones he decided to give it one final push into the darkness.

With every breath, the stagnant air felt like watery soup condensing at the back of his throat. He felt as if he was choking.

Up ahead he spotted a small hole barely wide enough to squeeze through. Should he continue or give up and go back to Anya? Even if he managed to clamber through the hole would he be able to turn around and get back out if he needed to? What could be on the other side? A dead-end most probably. So much danger – what was the point of taking such a risk?

With a sudden flash, the grey rat reappeared.

Like a guardian angel, it summoned Tom towards the narrow hole.

It had guided him before; was it doing the same again? Or this time was it leading him into some sort of an ambush?

Warily, he scraped along the floor of the tapering channel and gingerly pushed his face up to the dark hole. He found himself staring into a black void. Once again, there was no sign of the grey rat. Were his eyes playing tricks on him? He started to wonder if it had even been there at all, or had it just been his imagination?

Poking his moonstick into the gloom, all Tom could make out was a small chasm filled with shadows. Nothing but musty shadows. He watched carefully for signs of movement – nothing. He listened intently for any sounds – there were none. That was enough for Tom – he had finally come to the end. All his crawling and scrambling deep into the mountain had been a waste of time. His shoulders sagged; he sighed heavily; he felt like crying.

All he could think of was Anya waiting with her calf in the darkness. Now he had to go and tell her the bad news . . . they were trapped.

Slowly, he began to back away, but stopped when his beam of light accidentally landed on something shining more brightly than the crystal rocks surrounding it. A glinting cluster embedded in the wall, twinkling in the darkness. It looked just like a constellation of tiny stars encircled by gleaming rocks.

Tom squinted through the gloom. Had he found a seam of diamonds? Was he suddenly the richest boy in this distant galaxy? Would he be able to dislodge them and take them home in his rucksack? Would he ever find a way out of here? So many questions flowed through his brain. He decided to ignore the danger and investigate.

Coughing and gasping, with his chest rasping,

Tom Lennox dragged himself and his backpack through the tight gap. Slowly, he pulled himself along following the thin yellow light to the spot where the wall glistened.

Tom's face instantly broke into a wide smile. He had found something much more valuable to him right now than diamonds. It was snow! The first he had seen since his arrival. If the snow had blown in, he reasoned, this must be another way out of the cave. He began to scrape and before long, feeling the welcoming cool blast of fresh air on his face, Tom balled his gloved fist and punched a hole through the permafrost just large enough for him to scramble free.

THE JOURNEY BEGINS

The storm which had raged overnight had disappeared leaving a thick deposit of linen-white snow encrusted by frost.

Dawn was breaking as the sun began its weary climb through a cloud-dappled sky. It drizzled its pale light over the peaks of snow-laden mountains.

Tom crouched low to keep out of sight. After spending so much time in those dark tunnels, he screwed his eyes and waited for them to adjust to the daylight. Even though he had only just stepped out into the open air, he could already feel the coldness seeping through his boots and gloves.

He pulled his sister's garish scarf from the rucksack, wrapped it loosely around his neck and tucked it firmly out of sight. He briefly imagined Katie snuggling under her warm duvet back home and wondered if he had been wise to heed the wild calling of the wolves bringing him to such a cold, hostile, dangerous world.

Tugging the hood of his duffel coat forward to protect his ears from the biting wind, he set off in search of Anya's family following a deep channel carved into the snow by the overnight storm. On either side, lofty snowdrifts towered over him.

After a while, Tom came to a ledge high on the mountain which overlooked the main entrance to the cave. As he stared down, he could make out a single wolf shaking snow from its fur. Although there was no sign of the others, Tom knew the pack members would soon emerge from their frosty beds and resume their quest to break through to Anya and her calf.

He knew it was only a matter of time before they found a way in. He needed to act quickly to alert the other mammoths.

Meanwhile, inside the cave, Anya felt a welcoming draught of cold air refreshing her face. She wrapped her trunk around the sleeping calf and gently hugged her. 'Can you feel that cool breeze?' she whispered. The calf never opened her eyes. 'It means Little Bear must have found another way out. What a strange creature he was!' she murmured. She thought about his fantasy of being a time-adventurer. 'Hummmph, what nonsense!' she grunted. Could she really trust him to go and get help? She simply didn't know. But as Anya thought more about his incredible story, she started to doubt whether she would ever see him again.

All she could do for now was suckle her newborn calf and wait for Troyka to return. And while waiting, she would think of a name for her baby. Irena? No, Anya decided she wasn't keen on that name. Anastasia? Too long.

'Hey, I know,' she whispered softly to her baby. 'What about naming you after this cave? Crystal – hmmm, that's a lovely name.' She gazed down. 'Yes that's it, I think I'm going to call you Crystal!'

LEADER OF THE PACK?

Outside the cave entrance, Kirill shook the snow from his fur. The other wolves were still asleep; this gave him time to explore and do some thinking. Sniffing the cold morning air, his sensitive nose picked up a familiar scent wafting in the wind. He pawed frantically at the entrance and thrust his snout deep into the freshly fallen snow which had formed a seal around the great boulder. The odour reminded him of something – what was it? He sat down to scratch his ear, and then it came to him. 'I know that smell!' he murmured angrily.

He remembered that awful day – many moons ago, when he was just a puppy, his family had been attacked by humans. He had burrowed under the snow to hide and had watched helplessly as a tribe of hunters killed his mother Katya. His father had tried to defend her but there were too many men – too brutal. They beat his father with sticks and clubs and left him to die.

Kirill's mind went back to that terrible day. He remembered the shouting and the smell of those cruel men. That horrible, pungent tang of a human was in his nostrils then and now it had returned. His eyes blazed with anger.

But Kirill was also confused – what was a human doing inside the cave? How had he got in? Not to worry, as soon as he could find a way, he would have his revenge for what those men had done to his parents. He was certain of one thing: this human would provide extra food for his hungry pack.

But Kirill didn't know that deep inside the mountain, the small human he smelt had already wriggled his way to freedom through the labyrinth of tiny tunnels.

Once again the alpha wolf watched over his slumbering pack wrapped in their blankets of snow. He knew some were beginning to question whether he was still strong enough to be their leader. He had heard whispers and mutterings behind his back and felt he could no longer trust any of them.

Soon one of the younger males would challenge him to a fight. Kirill was secretly scared that if he lost that fight he would be cast out alone, betrayed by the mouths he had fed over many tough, lean years.

There were two other male dogs in the pack: their names were Flake and Prince. Flake was the weaker of the two – he wasn't too worried about him.

Kirill was certain that one day Prince would be the one to rise up and challenge his authority; he was young and stood out from the rest of the wolves because of his bright lemon eyes. Prince had always been the first to pick out signs of danger or spot a distant reindeer long before the others had smelt or seen it. His skills marked him out as a future pack leader. One day Prince would be his successor.

The wise old wolf watched warily as Prince slept. 'Your time hasn't come yet,' he whispered softly. 'Not while I'm strong enough to rule this pack. You'd do well to remember that I'm still the alpha male around here.' Pulling back his lips and wrinkling his nose in an ugly sneer, Kirill bared his fangs. 'You might be the Prince in the pack but if you try anything with me, I'll show you who is king,' he quietly growled.

As Kirill turned away, Prince warily opened

one eye – he had been awake all the time listening to every word. He wanted so much to leap up and challenge Kirill to a leadership fight. But something was troubling him: his keen sense of smell had also picked up Tom's scent. He lay puzzling why humans and mammoths were sharing the same space inside the cave – weren't they supposed to be sworn enemies? *No matter*, he thought, *there must be a way into that cave, and I'm going to find it!*

The temperature barely rose as the sun climbed slowly up into the sky. Kirill licked his freezing paws wondering how to squeeze past the entrance stone. He needed to show the other dogs he was strong in body and mind, and that he was still fit to lead them. He made a silent promise that today they would all have food.

A DECISION TO MAKE

'**S**zhcnuuuurrrrrggghhh'

'Oh Truba please shut up!' yelled Troyka.

'Szhcnuuuurrrrrggghhh!' juddered Truba even more loudly.

Troyka had been awake most of the night trying to block out the sound of Truba's snoring. 'Szhcnuuuurrrrrggghhh!' With his unusual wide-flared trunk, Truba was the loudest in the herd – even when he was awake! But his snores had shaken the branches overhead showering big dollops of snow all over the other mammoths. Luckily, the strong wind had swept the noises far into the forest – away from the ears of the alert, hungry wolves.

The overnight blizzard had disappeared leaving tall white stacks balancing unsteadily on the mountain peaks. But the wind was gaining strength once again, towing fresh snow-choked clouds across the sky.

Troyka was pondering how soon he should return to Crystal Cave to rescue Anya and her newborn calf. The wolves had fallen silent but that didn't mean they weren't close by. He was unaware that Kirill and his pack were waiting outside to ambush her. Had she given birth yet? Troyka didn't know.

He would put off going to the cave until tomorrow. One more day would make no difference – would it?

WIND OF CHANGE

U p on the mountain slope, Tom decided the best defence he had from the wolf pack was camouflage. His sister's coat blended in with the landscape even though it was streaked with dirt from crawling through tunnels. But her scarf was a real giveaway. He tucked it even further inside his coat to hide it from view. Luckily the stiff breeze blowing up from the valley was carrying Tom's scent away from the wolves rather than towards them.

He continued to crouch low, feeling the crusty

snow crunching softly beneath his boots. Slowly, he began to make his way down the mountain. Far below, he glimpsed the wolf pack pawing and sniffing outside the cave.

Dipping behind snowy ridges, he managed to keep out of sight but his progress was hampered by deep drifts swallowing his legs. He ploughed on, and soon arrived at the top of a slope which fell away steeply to a distant forest down in the valley. Below the tree line he could see an ice-coated lake shimmering in the pale sunlight.

Tom hoped that Anya's family were sheltering among the pines. He needed to get down to them as quickly as possible to warn them that Anya and her calf were in danger from a wolf attack. But Tom knew that as soon as he was out on the open slope, there would be nowhere to hide. If the wolves spotted him, he would be the one in danger – unless somehow he could plough through the snow faster than they could.

All of a sudden, the wind began to swirl and within seconds had changed direction, carrying Tom's scent down into the valley.

Immediately the wolves picked up the whiff of a human in their nostrils. They all began yapping excitedly. All except for Prince who bowed his head deep in thought.

How had that human escaped from the cave? he wondered.

Not realising that the wolves had picked up his own scent, Tom heard their distant barks. He hauled himself up to the peak of a small outcrop expecting to see the pack far below. Instead, as he raised his head to gain a better view, he found himself peering into a pair of dark brown eyes less than a metre away.

THE WISDOM OF PRINCE

Perfectly camouflaged, the white ptarmigan had blended into its background so well that Tom hadn't seen the bird until it was too late. For several seconds, they stared at each other with surprise until, with a startled squawk, the ptarmigan took off, its shrill alarm calls ringing out loud across the tundra.

The wolves were instantly alerted. Following the sound they jerked their heads to scan the mountain.

Kirill caught sight of Tom before he had chance to duck back behind the ridge. The old wolf leader quickly assessed the situation. *Hmm*, he thought, *this was no hefty beast but at least a snack was better than going another few days with an empty belly.* He signalled to the pack with three rapid yaps and they all set off in pursuit of the strange bear-like creature they had glimpsed.

The deadly chase was on as the wolves bounded upwards through the heavy snow.

Prince paused; pointing his muzzle high in the air, he instantly recognised the scent floating on the wind from the mountain ridge – it was the same he'd smelt inside the cave. *So there is another way out of that place*, he decided, *and if there was another way out, then there must be another way in.* He smiled smugly to himself. *Why hadn't Kirill and the rest of the wolves realised this too?* As he lowered his head, Prince curled his lip into a cruel lopsided sneer. All he had to do was find the secret entrance and the mammoths inside would be at his mercy. At last, the opportunity had come to overthrow Kirill as pack leader.

As the other wolves pressed on ahead, he called his best friend Nadiya back. She paused and looked at him uncertainly, unsure what she should do.

'Leave them, let them go,' he pleaded. 'Come with me instead. Kirill no longer knows what he is doing. he's not thinking clearly any more, he's too old to lead this wolf pack – too, erm, long in the fang you might say.'

Prince scoffed at his own joke. Then his face became serious again. 'Did you glimpse that tiny figure up on the mountain Nadiya? Couldn't you smell it? That was no bear, it was only a small human, a mere child – that's all. It won't fill your empty bellies, tonight you'll still be hungry. But I will deliver a proper meal, because now I'm sure there's another way into this cave – all we have to do is find it. Before night time comes this starving pack will turn against Kirill and I will become their king.'

Then he glared at her through the freshly falling snow and whispered softly, 'And if you join me Nadiya, you will be their queen.'

Nadiya shook her head defiantly. 'No Prince, you won't defeat Kirill – at least not yet, he's still too strong! Be patient, your time will come,' she told him soothingly. Nadiya turned away from Prince and set off to catch up with the pack, but she faltered and called back to him, 'Come with us Prince; let's stick together.'

Prince shook his head and turned away from her.

'Okay fine!' she hollered. 'You stay here if you want but—' Her final words were stolen by the wind.

Prince didn't know, but it was the last time he would ever hear Nadiya's voice. Nadiya didn't know, but it was the last time she would ever see him.

As Nadiya raced off to catch up with the pack,

Prince scowled; he felt she was betraying him.

'Okay!' he called after her. 'You stay loyal to Kirill if you must. I'll do this my way!'

But his words were whisked away on the wind – she never heard them.

Keeping his distance, Prince trotted behind the pack for a hundred metres or so then looped back towards the main cave entrance. Although the snow was thickening on the ground, he quickly spotted what he was looking for: the remains of an ancient path snaking between a thin clump of trees. He followed it and very soon began a steep, hazardous climb up the side of the mountain.

Two or three times Nadiya glanced over her shoulder hoping that Prince had changed his mind, but there was no sign of him. He had vanished.

Prince was sure he was doing the right thing by going alone. Even though none of the other wolves had noticed he had broken away from the pack, he was also sure they would thank him later when they had feasted on mammoth instead of that straggly man-child to fill their empty bellies. He followed the trail up the mountain until he spotted Tom's footprints in the snow.

PACK ATTACK

As soon as he realised the baying pack was onto him, Tom leapt to his feet. Could he escape from them? He pumped his legs, trying hard to run, but it was impossible in the deep snow. The wolves were closing on him. Anya's words kept returning,

'You'll never outrun a wolf Tom...they just keep coming.'

Tom's legs kept sinking into the deep snowdrifts. His situation was hopeless; he thought about putting on his goggles and returning to his warm, cosy bed. But that meant abandoning Anya inside the mountain – no he could never do that. His legs carried on pumping through the snow but he was going nowhere.

Kirill sensed victory; as he got closer, he could see that his quarry was a young human – a boy. 'That will make the kill even more enjoyable,' he mumbled angrily. 'I will finally get my revenge for what those cruel men did to my parents.'

Kirill commanded the pack to split into two groups – the classic wolf-hunting strategy. Six dogs crept towards their target from the right flank while the remaining five positioned themselves beneath the man-child to prevent him from fleeing downhill.

Kirill knew the boy had no chance of getting away.

As the wolves slowly advanced towards him, Tom could see they were struggling to haul themselves out of the deep drifts. He thought about trying to run up into the mountain but he knew there was no way he could beat them to its snow-laden summit.

'You'll never outrun a wolf Tom.' Anya seemed to be whispering in his ear again.

Within minutes the wolves had encircled him. Now it was too late to do anything. Tom realised with fear in his eyes that he had no chance of joining Anya's family in the forest.

Howling, snapping, snarling, with bared teeth the pack inched savagely towards him. They were now so close, Tom could see the hair standing up on the ridges of their backs. Saliva dripped from their gasping, greedy lips. Breath-vapour ballooned from their mouths in the cold morning air.

SILENT ASSASSIN

High above in her dark lair, the lean sabre-toothed tiger listened to the excited yapping of the wolves as she dragged her rough tongue over the kittens' soft, velvety fur. Saiba could feel their thin skin rippling over their tiny bones; she knew they desperately needed food. But there was nothing she could give them apart from a few precious drops of milk, and even that was running out. If they didn't eat soon she feared they would starve to death.

Saiba crept out from the shadows to peer down

at the wolves surrounding a curious small bear-like creature, when out of the corner of her narrow topaz-coloured eyes she caught sight of something moving with incredible stealth beneath the ridge. She had spotted a lone wolf which had sneaked away from the pack. She watched curiously as it followed a trail of footprints leading to a fresh mound of snow.

Prince had no idea that two sharp eyes were locked on to every move he now made. He approached the small hole in the ground with no inkling that his own life was hanging in the balance.

Even though she remained invisible to Prince, Saiba was wary. *Why had a single wolf broken away from the rest of its pack?* she wondered. 'No matter, this could be my last chance to keep my little cubs alive,' she purred softly.

Saiba was a fearless cat: she knew she could overpower a single wolf. 'Stay where you are little kittens,' she whispered. 'No crying out for me while I'm away. You must promise to keep quiet or the wolf dogs will take you. I will be back soon with food.'

She slipped silently from her ledge.

Prince glanced several times over his shoulder at Kirill leading his dogs towards the small human. He shook his head. 'Why can't those fools see they are closing in on little more than a morsel?' he scoffed.

He lowered his head into the opening and sniffed. His sensitive nose soon picked up remains of the scent left behind by Tom. He also caught a waft of Anya's musty smell from deep inside the cave.

Prince's sharp nose also told him that a newly

born calf lurked in there – somewhere.

He began to plan his attack. The calf would be weak and defenceless but not its mother who would fight ferociously to defend her baby. He would do well to avoid her spiky tusks and trampling feet.

Prince took one final look at the baying pack of wolves surrounding the man-child before squeezing through the gap. But he failed to notice the Siberian tiger springing down from her lofty ledge 100 metres above him.

Saiba glared at the lone wolf thrusting his head into the snow before he cautiously disappeared into the hole. Crouching low, she crept slowly and silently towards the tiny entrance.

Once inside, Prince clambered along a narrow passageway. Although he could see nothing in the eerie darkness, his nostrils were soon filled with the fresh, inviting smell of mammoth which told him he was on the right trail. The only sound came from his own claws jangling on the polished rocks.

Seconds later Saiba slipped through the same snow hole. She quickly picked up the mammoths' scent and followed it, but there was something far sweeter in the air, something much more appetising: a tasty meal for her kittens.

As Saiba's eyes quickly adjusted to the darkness, she soon had the wolf in her sights. Prince never heard her creeping silently behind on the feather-soft pads of her feet.

As he clattered clumsily along the thin corridor, Prince had no idea Saiba was stalking him – until she leapt on his back. Her claws sprang out gripping his body tightly. He howled in pain and his legs began to buckle. There was a brief tussle. She sank her long curved fangs deep into his neck and he slumped lifelessly to the ground.

Saiba released her grip of Prince's body, satisfied that her family would eat well tonight. She licked her crimson lips with delight; the kill had been oh, so easy. Now for the hard part: firmly clenching the wolf's bushy tail between her teeth, she slowly dragged the carcass backwards through the tunnel.

The grey rat, accustomed to the darkness, had witnessed the savage kill. It scampered off shaking its head as Prince was hauled away.

ROLL AWAY THE STONE

Anya was bored. She shuffled uncomfortably in the dark cave listening to the small creatures clicking and clacking over the stone floor beside her. Blindly, she probed with her trunk, lifted a wriggling, squirming beetle, popped it into her mouth and munched contentedly – CRUNCH!

In her silent world she realised she could no longer hear the wolves scraping and scratching at the mouth of the cave. *Maybe they've finally given up and moved on,* she thought. Then she heard Prince's anguished cry from somewhere deep inside the maze of tunnels. She had no idea he had been attacked by Saiba. Instead, she wondered if the pack had found a way in through the entrance opened up by Little Bear. She held her breath listening for any telltale sounds that the cave had been invaded. If she was right they would soon find their way to her chamber.

Anya began to panic: she knew she would not be able to fight off a hungry wolf pack. She scrambled uneasily to her feet, wondering if she could try to move the big boulder all by herself. *After all*, she thought, *Troyka had done it. How hard could it really be?*

She inhaled deeply, put her shoulder against the stone and pushed with all her strength. It didn't budge. It was much harder than Troyka had made it seem. She grimaced and thrust again but it remained firmly wedged. Breathing heavily, she decided to give it one final try. She locked her powerful hind legs against the cave wall and shunted rhythmically against the boulder until it gradually began to rock from side to side. The little calf watched as her mother bellowed and strained.

'You can help me if you want!' grunted Anya.

Before long, the two of them were heaving as hard as they could until they felt the stone start to roll away.

Moments later they had opened up a gap just wide enough to squeeze through. As daylight flooded into Crystal Cave, the calf caught sight of something gleaming on the ground next to her discarded blanket. She scooped it up with the tip of her trunk.

Anya was met by a sprinkling of snowflakes as she slipped through the gap. She moistened her dry mouth by sucking on a chunk of ice and watched with pride as her young calf stepped out onto the freezing snow for the first time. The young mammoth's eyes filled with wonder as she stared at the snow-clad mountains in the distance and the ice-covered lake nestling in the valley far below. The two mammoths filled their lungs with the fresh mountain air as Anya held her trunk over the youngster's eyes to shield them from the glinting sun.

'Quick, help me to roll the stone back in case the wolves are already inside the cave!' pleaded Anya.

Together, they heaved and gasped until the boulder once again plugged the hole in the mountain.

SLIP SLIDING AWAY

On the sloping glacier the wolves had now formed a circle around Tom. They had him fully surrounded. He was desperately trying to work out a solution – was there even a solution at all? 'I mustn't give up,' he muttered to himself.

'*You'll never outrun a wolf Tom, they just keep coming.*' Those words again! But why did they keep echoing? It was as if Anya was reaching out to him – but what was she trying to tell him?

He looked up at the moon refusing to leave

the cloud-dappled sky. Then some more of Anya's words came to him; what had she called his torch? A *'moonstick!'* All at once an idea began to form. Weren't wolves scared of fire? Yes, he was sure they were – all animals were. If he could fool them into believing the light from his own moonstick was an actual flame he might be able to ward them off. But how long could it keep them at bay? He didn't know but at least it was worth a try.

Slipping off his rucksack he took it out, looped the thin strap over his wrist, and pointed it at six wolves creeping towards him. But the pale beam was hopelessly weak in the daylight. They simply ignored it and kept advancing.

Tom's situation was now so desperate he realised he was faced with no choice but to save his own life. With the wolves about to overwhelm him, he decided to put on his headset and vanish before they attacked.

With frozen fingers he reached for his backpack, turned it over in the snow and began to open it. As he fumbled with the zip, the pack slipped from his grasp and began to slide away on the steep snowy bank.

'Hey not so fast!' Tom grabbed the straps. 'So fast . . .' he repeated the words slowly as he gripped the bag. The wolves were less than 50 metres away. He could feel their presence behind him, but he didn't dare cast a glance over his shoulder in case it incited them to attack.

Although his thoughts were in a whirl, Anya's advice kept repeating,

'You'll never outrun a wolf Tom, you'll never outrun a wolf ...' What relevance did those words have right now?

Then it dawned on him; he realised what her whispered words were trying to tell him. She was right: of course he could never outrun a wolf. He didn't even need to try. Now he felt sure there was another way to escape. He had the answer right there in his hands.

Hmmm, he thought, *was it possible?* As he sat clutching his blue rucksack, a smile spread across his face – even though the snarling, snapping wolves were closing in fast.

'Maybe I can't outrun them Anya,' he yelled at the top of his voice. 'But I can definitely outsledge them!'

He slipped the bag underneath his bottom and began to paddle forwards with his hands. With a powerful shove he tried to propel himself down the mountain slope but the backpack sunk beneath his weight into the snow. Oh no, now he knew he was in real trouble. Had it been his last chance of escape? Not quite. There was another way. There was always another way.

He raised himself from the shallow he had created, then set the blue bag down in front of him. Once again it began to slide downhill but this time he had planned for that to happen and he was ready. Just as it started to build up speed, he dived headfirst, launching himself onto his backpack. He was off, skimming rapidly over the snow like a flat pebble flung across the surface of a pond.

Feeling every bump beneath the flimsy fabric of his bag he barrelled into the startled wolves, skittling the pack. Kirill lunged and caught hold of Tom's

coat but the makeshift sled was travelling too fast for the fearsome wolf to hold on. The fabric tore from Kirill's slavering mouth leaving him with nothing but a few strands of cloth dangling from his bared teeth.

TOM'S FROSTY RECEPTION

By the time the dogs turned to chase the boy down the mountain, he was almost out of sight. But starving wolves don't give up easily. With tails wagging excitedly, they bounded after their rapidly-disappearing prey.

Faster and faster went Tom as he bounced down the icy slope. Glancing back, he could see he had left the wolves far behind. Worryingly, they had regrouped and were already beginning to follow the shallow track made by his crude bobsleigh.

Tom was now hurtling at a dangerous speed. Ahead, he could make out a cluster of brown shapes shuffling between the trees at the edge of the forest. He broke into a broad smile as the shapes loomed larger; it was Anya's family. Using his arms and legs he steered towards them. But Tom knew he was putting the mammoths in peril by leading the wolves straight to them. Too late to do anything about that now, he had to alert Troyka and tell him that Anya and her calf were safe.

Digging his heels into the snow left deep gouges as he hurtled towards the trees but it did little to slow him down. Tom blended into the snowy background so perfectly, the mammoths never saw him careering towards them until he slammed into Truba. The collision was so powerful it knocked the large mammoth off his feet. Tom, dazed by the impact with the great beast, began to brush the snow from his clothes. Groggily, he tried to stand up but was swiftly pinned down by one of Troyka's long curved tusks. It rested like a pirate's curved cutlass across the boy's throat.

Tom gawped at the huge mammoth angrily thrusting his head from side to side looking as if it was preparing to attack. Whereas Anya had been huge, the beast now towering over him was simply enormous, standing at around five metres tall with a mane of dishevelled hair waving wildly in the wind like burnt barley. 'Yyyou mmmust be TTTroyka,' he stuttered nervously. He turned his head towards the other mammoth he had crashed into. Instantly, he knew it was Truba by his large flared trunk. He was also huge, but, despite his overwhelming size, the dazed mammoth remained on the ground.

'Are you alright?' Tom asked tenderly. 'Anya said I might bump into you, but I don't think she meant I would actually bump into you like that – sorry, Truba!'

As soon as he heard Anya's name, Troyka immediately calmed down, withdrawing his tusk from Tom's throat. 'Who are you? Where have you come from? And how do you know Anya?' he asked. 'Is she safe?'

'She's fine, I promise you. Oh, by the way, my name is Tom Lennox.'

Troyka eyed him suspiciously. 'You can't possibly have seen Anya, I know that because I left her hiding in a sealed cave. You had better not have rolled away the stone, she needed it there to keep safe and warm.'

Winnie pushed herself between Troyka and Tom. 'Don't be stupid, Troyka!' she snorted. 'Look at the size of him ... how do you think this little bear could possibly move that giant boulder all by himself?'

She stared into Tom's eyes. 'Now please tell us honestly – how did you meet Anya?'

'Will everyone please stop calling me Little Bear!' shrilled Tom. 'Anya called me that too. Even though you think I look like one, I'm not a bear at all – look!' Once again he untoggled his coat to reveal the mammoth motif on his jumper.

Tom realised the mammoths would never believe how he had come to be with them. He took a deep breath before explaining how he had travelled through time – from an identical but much warmer planet far away across the universe.

He tried to sound convincing as he told them how he had met Anya inside a cave high up in the mountain.

With bewildered expressions and breath-vapour streaming from their trunks, the mammoths listened carefully but couldn't decide whether they should believe him or not.

'Okay then,' said Winnie with an impatient sigh.

'If what you say is true – which I very much doubt – then please explain how you were able to enter the sealed cave.'

Hmm, how indeed? thought Tom. *They would only be confused if I told them I arrived inside the cave through a time portal.* So to avoid confusing them even more, he secretly crossed his fingers and told them a little fib: 'I, er, found a tiny secret entrance into the cave. It was the same one I crawled out of to come here,' he added. Then, with a broad smile, he told the mammoths that not only had he met Anya, he had also seen her baby.

Their eyes lit up when they heard that the calf had been born.

'She is ready to leave Crystal Cave,' he said joyfully, but then his face became stern. 'There is something else you all must know – Anya and her calf were being hounded by wolves camped outside the entrance but they spotted me when I tried to sneak away. They followed me down the mountain. They'll be here in a few minutes.'

'A few minutes! What does that even mean?' asked Berta.

Tom realised the mammoths had no idea what a minute or even an hour was. 'It means the wolves will be here very soon,' he told Berta firmly. 'In fact, look!' He pointed his finger at the glacier.

The mammoths gazed up at the mountain looming overhead. On the distant slopes they could see grey shapes beetling towards them.

'Quick into the forest!' bellowed Berta. 'Follow me!'

'No!' With a shake of her head, Winnie signalled she was unsure. Her splintered tusk waved defiantly. 'The wolves will follow us and they will be able to pass between the trees more swiftly than we can.'

'Well what do you suggest then – that we climb the trees to escape from the wolves?' sneered Berta sarcastically.

'Maybe we could fight them off,' suggested Truba. 'How many are there Tom?'

'Erm ten, eleven or perhaps twelve. I'm not sure. I never thought to count them.'

'Hmm, then we're greatly outnumbered. Maybe fighting them isn't such a good idea after all,' said Truba solemnly.

'Well maybe we can run up the mountain side,' Winnie suggested.

'And then what?' uttered Berta. 'Surely the wolves will follow us wherever we go!'

They began mumbling to each other until Tom stepped between them and cleared his throat. 'Ahem. Can I say something?' They stopped murmuring and nodded.

'You will never outrun a wolf,' he said.

The mammoths looked expectantly as if waiting for more wise words – but there were none.

'Er, that's it!' yelled Tom with a shrug. 'You will never outrun a wolf.'

Troyka grinned. 'You sound just like Anya, she is always telling us that.'

'Yes, I know, it was what she told me just before I left her in the cave – and now I know she was right,' he said sternly. 'I wouldn't have got away from them if it hadn't been for this.' He held up his backpack to show them.

'Yes, but we can't all climb on board that thing!' said Winnie scornfully. 'So we'll have to take our chances and run. Even wolves can't move very quickly in deep snow, everyone knows that.'

Berta nodded wisely.

'I'm afraid it's too late to think about running up

mountains,' screamed Troyka. 'Look!' He pointed his great trunk up the glacier. They turned and stared. The wolves were bearing down towards them. Now, less than 600 metres away, time was quickly running out for the mammoth family.

'Well then!' shrieked Tom. 'If we can't go to the mountain, then the mountain will have to come to us.'

They all turned and stared at him as if he had suddenly gone bonkers.

BLOW YOUR OWN TRUMPET

'I'm serious!' yelled Tom.

'That's ridiculous!' chorused the mammoths. 'Mountains can't walk!'

'Normally they can't,' agreed Tom calmly. 'But I think Crystal Mountain might.' He pointed to the summit where a thick dark cloud hovered menacingly over its beautiful snow-capped peak.

'How can we make it do that?' screamed Winnie.

'Simply by hollering at it!'

'What? You're telling us to shout at a mountain?'

'Not just shout,' cried Tom. 'I want you to bellow as loudly as you can. Trust me,' he added earnestly. 'Faith can move mountains.'

'But there's no one here called Faith,' whispered Truba to Winnie. She shook her head and gave him a hefty shove.

'You're talking about an avalanche aren't you?' asked Troyka glumly. Tom nodded.

Winnie was well aware of the dangers of falling snow. 'Have you ever seen an avalanche?' she asked him earnestly.

Tom didn't reply.

'Well we have,' she said. 'And they are truly terrifying!'

Truba swept his head decisively from side to side. 'I agree with Winnie!' he said.

'Me too!' added Berta.

'No! No way, it's far too dangerous!' said Truba firmly.

'And wolves aren't?' Tom gazed into each of the

mammoths' eyes. 'Look I know my plan is stupid, I know it is really dangerous, I know it might not even work at all, but if...' He noticed Truba was about to interrupt but Tom held up his hand defiantly...'if it works,' he continued, 'a deep fall of snow could cut us off from the wolves and we'll be safe. If we are lucky it might even sweep them away altogether.'

'Yeah, and if we're unlucky, it'll sweep us away too,' said Winnie.

They all nodded silently.

'Maybe you're right,' said Berta calmly. 'But what if Tom is right? What if his plan is our only chance of getting out of here alive?'

Before any of them could answer Berta's question, a bone-chilling sound rang out across the glacier. 'Whhooooohhh'... The wolves were howling throatily – they had chosen their victim.

Neither the mammoths nor Tom knew who had

been singled out by the wolves, but if they didn't act fast, they would find out very soon!

At that moment a dark cloud hovered menacingly over the towering peak of Crystal Mountain. A fierce electrical storm was brewing.

'Okay, it's worth a try!' shouted Truba. 'Let's do it now or we'll be too late. Look!'

The mammoths turned to follow the direction of Truba's outstretched trunk. By now the wolves were only 300 metres away, but their progress had slowed as they struggled to make their way through the deep drifts.

The mammoths huddled together shaking their heads.

'Many times we've seen the destructive power of avalanches,' said Winnie. 'Once they are in full flow, nothing can stop them. If we agree to do it, how can you guarantee we will be safe?'

Tom held out his hands, palms upwards, and

shrugged his shoulders. He didn't have an answer.

Truba, Winnie and Berta glanced at each other – uncertain what they should do.

Meanwhile the wolves were slowly getting closer. Once again, they had separated into two hunting parties as they prepared themselves to attack.

Finally, Troyka spoke. 'We agree!' he said reluctantly.

As soon as Tom had outlined his plan, they all turned to face the mountain. The mammoths raised their trunks towards the snow-laden peak, took deep breaths and bellowed in unison. Tom joined in by shouting as hard as he could but his voice was drowned out by thunderous booming that came from the herd. Tom put his hands over his ears as he yelled. Carefully, he scanned the mountain hoping for movement but there was none.

Less than 100 metres to the west, the panting

wolves were slowly gaining ground. They had singled out Winnie, and were now stalking towards her. They knew the other mammoths would form a circle to defend her but the wolves planned to scatter them all by attacking from different directions.

As they approached the herd, Kirill parted his dry lips and sneered to himself. He would provide food for his hungry pack and prove to them he was still a worthy leader. He could hear the loud calls of the mammoths, but he had heard these pitiful cries so many times before his pack attacked. He was sure that the beasts were panicking, screaming for help.

But Kirill was mistaken. The shrill cries he was listening to were the mammoths beckoning snow from the mountain's peak.

The mammoths blew and bellowed stridently, but it made no difference; Crystal Mountain refused to give up its snowload.

Tom lowered his
hands and turned to them as they gasped
for breath. 'You might as well stop!' he wheezed. 'My
plan isn't working. I'm sorry I've let you all down.'

The next moment the air around them was ripped open by the loudest sound Tom had ever heard, 'PHHHEEEEUUUURRRRRGGGGHHHHH!!'

Once again Tom threw his hands up to his ears to block out the terrible noise. Trees began to tremble and a violent tremor spread through the icy earth. Instantly Tom thought an avalanche had begun, but he was confused because the sound was not coming from the mountain.

The marauding wolves stopped for a moment and stared. The raucous blast shuddered across the tundra. Everyone turned to look where it was coming from.

It was Truba! With his eyes firmly closed in concentration, his feet planted deep into the snow and his great flared trunk jutting out like an alpine horn, the great mammoth was blowing hard. And just when it seemed he could blow no more, he pushed out his chest, gulped more air into his lungs and began again. Only this time, Truba's snorting roar was even louder, as clouds of breath-vapour billowed from his flared nostrils.

'PHHHEEEEUUUURRRRRGGGHHHH!!'

SNOW, SNOW FASTER

Tom turned and scanned the horizon. Thick black clouds were colliding above the mountain's summit. He blinked rapidly as thin tongues of lightning flicked out, licking the snowy peak as if it were a giant ice cream.

A loud thunderclap rocked the mountain towering magnificently above them, causing its snowy cap to slide several metres before coming to rest overhanging a steep rock face.

Finally, Truba collapsed. All that blowing had

made him dizzy. As he sank to his knees, he failed to hear the sharp blast of thunder that had exploded over the summit.

Troyka, Winnie and Berta turned and looked hopefully at the mountain. They were dismayed to see it was still intact.

'I've failed,' gasped Truba mournfully, as he slowly scrambled to his feet.

'No, we all failed,' said Troyka solemnly. 'It wasn't only you Truba, we all tried to bring down the snow.'

'Quick, run for it!' screamed Winnie, 'Follow me into the forest, it's our last chance!'

But they were too late. A small party of wolves had circled behind the mammoths to cut off their escape. Tom and the herd were totally surrounded. Everything went quiet. Then out of the silence came the strangest sound,

'Phhffissstt.'

The wolves were about to pounce on Winnie when they stopped to listen. They looked at each other in bewilderment. Instantly the mammoths realised it was the softly spoken mountain murmuring a simple word of hope to them.

'Phhffissstt' it whispered again – and then again, as large chunks of the snowy peak crumbled and began to slide away. The summit was finally releasing its deadly cargo – slowly at first, but quickly gathering speed.

Within seconds a white foaming tsunami was roaring downhill.

'Yes! I did it!' screamed Truba excitedly.

But the others gazed in horror. The avalanche was heading straight towards them.

MOUNTAIN RESCUE

Triumph was rapidly turning to terror as the wave hurtled downhill. Millions of tonnes of ice and snow gushed angrily, drowning out the squeals of terrified, whimpering wolves who were simply swallowed up by the white tide and swept away.

Desperate to flee from the dissolving mountain, the mammoths headed for the dense forest as uprooted trees collapsed all around. Troyka and Truba disappeared among the pines, closely followed by Berta.

But Tom and Winnie were not so lucky, they found their path cut off by the plunging snow.

Now their only hope was to outrun the avalanche, but Tom slipped and fell as he tried to launch himself towards the trees. Winnie began moving swiftly downhill, stopping only when she heard Tom's desperate scream above the thunderous roar, 'Yeeeaaaaaaaarrrrrgghhhh.' She turned round to find him sprawled on the frozen ground.

Tilting her head towards the mountain, Winnie watched helplessly as the unstoppable mass bulldozed towards her.

Berta had also heard Tom's screech; faltering at the edge of the forest, she was unsure what she should do or even what she *could* do. She thought about going back to help but that meant trying to cross the dangerous, fast-flowing river of snow.

As the fringe of the avalanche reached Tom, he

was sure he was about to sink beneath it forever. He cowered and braced himself for the full impact. It didn't happen.

Curiously, he watched the snow cascading over him like a winter waterfall. Solid white rivers gushed on either side, yet miraculously, Tom was untouched. How? Why? He risked a glance over his shoulder. Towering above him was Berta, courageously risking her own life to protect him.

With her feet planted firmly apart she had formed a shield to save Tom from the onrushing snow. But Berta knew her strength would not hold back the torrent for long. Tom knew that she could have scampered into the forest but bravely, unselfishly, she had chosen to stay and help him.

Although Berta was incredibly powerful, her strength was nothing compared to the mighty force unleashed from Crystal Mountain. Her body tilted towards Tom. If not by the snow, then surely the mammoth would soon topple and crush the small boy.

Tom felt his arm being wrenched as Winnie stepped defiantly into the eye of the avalanche and snatched him away.

Unlike Berta, Winnie had no intention of hanging about. She coiled her trunk like a thick snake around Tom's body, gripped him tightly, and pulled him towards her through the choking swirling snowcloud.

Tom could make out the blurred outlines of several wolves bobbing and somersaulting past him, their terrified whelps drowned out by the thunderous roar of the avalanche and the cracking and splintering of trees.

Just as the avalanche started to wrap itself around them like a cold clammy duvet, Winnie rose up and with a powerful flick of her trunk, she scooped Tom up,

raised him high into the air, then she ran for their lives.

UNEASY RIDER

Troyka had no idea of the drama that was unfolding on the mountain slope behind him. He crashed among the pines believing he was leading everyone to safety. He was sure they would all be secure among the stronger, thicker trees in the heart of the forest.

Pausing, he looked behind to see Truba puffing and gasping. But where were the others? With horror, Troyka realised that the avalanche must have swallowed them up. 'Stop Truba, we must go back and help them!' he screamed.

By the time the two mammoths returned to the rapidly vanishing tree line, they could only watch helplessly as Winnie galloped down towards the frozen lake with the boy riding on her back, grasping desperately at her hair.

'Quick – come on!' yelled Truba. 'We've got to help her.' They bounded after Winnie through the surging snow.

Tom was struggling to hold on to Winnie. He grabbed handfuls of her coarse hair and clutched it tightly as she bolted forward trying to outrun the avalanche. But Winnie's hair was wet and slippery; it felt like squelchy seaweed as it slid between his frozen fingers.

As she surged and weaved between rough chunks of ice, Tom thrust out his legs and squeezed hard trying to grip her shoulders between his knees to stop himself from being buffeted, but the mammoth's body was too wide. As she twisted and lurched between tumbling trees and blocks of ice, Tom somersaulted over her head and plunged downwards into the icy cauldron.

Just as the snow was about to gobble him up, Tom's flailing, desperate hands grabbed the jagged end of something long and smooth. At first he imagined he had taken hold of a tumbling icicle torn from a frozen waterfall until he felt it lift him high above the choking morass of snow which was clogging his mouth and lungs. He caught a fleeting glimpse of Winnie's face and realised he had grasped her broken tusk.

In the same way that mountaineers find tiny fissures in a rock face to hold on, the numb fingers of Tom's left hand searched for finger holds among the protruding filaments of the tusk, whilst his right hand clamped on to the shaft of gleaming ivory and latched on. He was determined not to let go.

Onwards they surged down the crumbling mountain pursued by the two male mammoths.

The avalanche plunged after them.

Tom was surprised that a mammoth could move so quickly. Breathing heavily, she galloped ahead of the great white wave, easily outpacing the fast-flowing snow but she was weakening and eventually, began to slow down. Soon the chasing avalanche started to overtake Winnie, it wrapped itself around her, sapping the remaining strength from her legs. A cloud of snow slid beneath the mammoth, tossing her high in the air.

The gushing cascade carried them down the glacier, rolling and tumbling as if they were in a giant snowglobe. Down it ploughed to the fringes of the glittering lake, pushing Tom and Winnie out onto the frozen surface.

Gradually, the avalanche slowed to a trickle as

the last fragments of snow, rocks and broken trees skated onto the ice and came to rest beside them.

Shivering with cold in soaking wet clothes, Tom opened his eyes to find Winnie lying next to him. The roaring mountain had finally fallen silent. She was breathing heavily but she had survived. Though buffeted, battered and bruised, thankfully no bones were broken.

Tom was relieved to see Troyka and Truba panting and gasping as they stood at the edge of the lake only a few metres away.

BREAKING GLASS

Frozen and frightened, Tom pulled himself to his feet. He opened his mouth to thank Winnie for saving his life, but stopped when he heard a chilling sound like ice cubes being dropped into a glass of warm water, cliiiink cliiiiick pliiink. He looked down as a crinkled cobweb of cracks spread out from underneath the mammoth's bulky body. More and more of them. The bowing ice was breaking apart.

The lake's crust had become a fragile plate of splintered glass buckling beneath the weight of

Winnie, and the boulders and trees strewn all around her. Now they were both in danger of plunging into the freezing water.

Troyka immediately recognised the danger. He remembered the day he had fallen through the same ice when he was a young mammoth and how lucky he had been to escape with his life. 'Quick Winnie!' he screamed. 'Get up or you'll – '

His warning came too late. With a chilling noise, the ice began to split apart Kerrreecchhh!

A large hole opened up, and Winnie plunged in.

Tom watched in horror as she disappeared. 'No Winnie, no!' he yelled.

They stood gawping at the hole fearing that she had gone forever. Instantly, ice crystals started crawling across the rippled water. A scab was forming on the surface; the lake was already beginning to heal itself.

Tom feared that Winnie might become trapped underneath when all of a sudden the water started churning and moments later she bobbed up like a cork between the fractured ice. Her front legs pawed desperately at the splintered surface as she fought to keep her head above water.

She shuddered violently, gasping for breath with

cold-water shock as the lake closed around her body, trying to suck her down into its dark depths.

Although Winnie was only a few metres from the shore, the shattered shards of ice made it impossible for her to scramble to safety.

With little time to act before the lake's cold crust broke up completely,   Tom briskly rubbed his hands together, trying to pump some warmth and feeling into his frozen fingers. He unravelled the scarf from his neck, rapidly tied a crude knot at each end, and unfurled it towards his friend. 'Here Winnie!' he roared. 'Grab this!'

Obediently, the startled mammoth spread her floppy trunk onto the ice next to Tom. She took hold of the scarf and gripped it firmly.

'Hold on as tightly as you can!' he screamed. 'And don't let go.'

He flung the other end of the scarf to Truba. 'Try hauling her towards you!' he shouted. He was confident that Truba would be strong enough to pull her to safety, but doubtful whether a woollen scarf could take the weight of a fully grown mammoth.

Tom and Troyka held their breath as Truba wrapped his trunk around the end of the scarf and tugged with all his strength while Winnie desperately held on.

But the harder Truba yanked, the longer the scarf became, until it looked like a tattered rope which was getting thinner and thinner as it stretched out tautly between the two mammoths.

Tom felt sure the scarf would snap at any moment. 'Come on Truba, pull harder!' The scene resembled a weird titanic tug o' war. He watched tensely as the great mammoth strained with all his might. 'Harder, Truba, harder!'

Finally, Truba dug his heels deep into the snow, arched his back, and with supreme effort, slowly towed Winnie through the broken ice to the water's edge.

Tom let out a 'whoop' of delight as he watched her scramble onto the shore. But he failed to notice that the lake was trying to swallow him up too. He hadn't spotted the cracks that were spreading out under his own feet. All of a sudden he found himself wobbling unsteadily on a thick pane of ice that had broken free. He knew his life would be in danger if he fell into the paralysing cold water.

AFTER-SHOCK

Troyka noticed Tom was in trouble. The giant mammoth risked his own safety by bravely stepping out onto the lake which instantly began to yield beneath his vast weight. He flicked out his trunk. 'Jump towards me now!' he bawled.

As Tom launched himself towards Troyka's outstretched trunk, his foot slipped into the freezing water which spilled into his boot and quickly seeped through his thick woollen sock. The coldness held Tom's toes in an ice-like grip, making him grimace and shriek with pain.

With the water sucking hard at his boot, Tom managed to pull his leg free from the lake but the boot was gone. He glimpsed it sinking silently down into the murky depths.

Troyka urgently grabbed hold of Tom with the tip of his trunk and with the ice breaking up all around him, he bolted to safety.

Truba was still trying to recover his breath but found enough energy to lunge forward at the edge of the lake and thrust his enormous trunk into the water. He fished around for several seconds before hoisting the dripping boot from the swirl.

Although Winnie was numbed by her dip in the cold lake, she heard Tom's teeth chattering and noticed him shivering. She twisted and shook herself dry before wrapping her trunk around him. Lovingly, she cradled him up to her face and poured her soft, warm breath over his frozen body. Then, ever so tenderly, she licked his hands with her rough tongue to restore some warmth into his frozen fingers. 'Thanks for saving me,' she said tenderly.

Tom shrugged. 'No need to thank me, Truba was the one who pulled you from the lake.'

'Yes, that's true, but if it weren't for your quick thinking with this!' she held up the thin tattered scarf and passed it back to him.

'I don't know what my sister Katie will say when she sees it!' he mumbled as he stuffed the scarf into his backpack.

All of a sudden, a worried expression began to spread across Troyka's face. 'Something's not right here,' he said calmly.

Truba nodded. 'Yeah, you're right Troyka, something's missing, but what?'

They all gazed around them pondering what was

wrong; then all at once they bellowed, 'Berta!'

'Where did she go?' asked Truba. 'The last time I saw her was up on the mountain.' He carefully scanned the glacier hoping to see Berta lumbering down towards him over the snowy debris. But there was no sign of her.

'Wait! I remember now,' added Truba. 'She was running right behind me when the avalanche crashed into us.'

'Yes, she was,' said Winnie. 'But she stopped to help Tom when he slipped. Then I lost sight of her. I thought she'd followed us down the mountain.'

'Well she's not here is she?' sighed Truba. 'And that can mean only one thing . . . she's somewhere under all that snow,' he added sadly.

Where to start? Within seconds the mammoths were desperately probing the newly churned snow with their long curved tusks feeling for signs of Berta's soft body. Tom could see their task was hopeless. He suspected the mammoths also knew they had little chance of finding her, but they carried on searching until the sun slipped over the mountain peaks leaving a trail of liquid gold shimmering on the shattered lake.

THE SEARCH CONTINUES

After resting briefly, they were guided by the pale glow of the moon to carry on digging. They each called out to Berta hoping for a sign that she had somehow survived. But the only sound in the desolate brutal landscape was the whispering wind rummaging through the few trees that remained.

They searched in the moonlight but found nothing. Their hopes of finding Berta were raised every time a tusk pressed into something soft beneath the snow, but all they uncovered were the crushed bodies of wolves. There was no sign of her.

The exhausted mammoths finally settled down to rest. Above them, a billion stars twinkled in the silent skies.

'Try and get some sleep,' Troyka told them. 'We'll start looking again first thing in the morning.'

Tom snuggled into Winnie's fur, marvelling at the slender moon casting its ghostly glow upon the glacier. Truba had fallen asleep straight away and was already snoring loudly.

Winnie followed Tom's gaze up to the jewelled night. 'Is your family really somewhere out there like you told us?' she whispered.

'Yes,' he replied. 'They live on a planet like this, except it's much warmer there. In fact, some say it's getting too warm!'

'Ooh, I can't imagine what it must feel like to be too warm,' she told him with a frown. 'Show me where they live.'

He held out his hand towards a vague smattering of light. 'Somewhere among that faint cluster of stars over there,' he said, stretching out a finger. 'We call that cream-coloured light the Milky Way.'

Winnie squinted at the freckled universe. '"Milky way"' she repeated with a smile. 'Mmmm sounds dreamy. But show me exactly where you live Tom,' she begged him. 'I would love to meet your family; even though your sister has a strange taste in clothes!' She tugged playfully at the toggles of Katie's duffel coat.

They peered into the void as Tom pointed at a dim light flickering vaguely in a distant constellation.

'Somewhere over there, you can just make out a tiny star – I think that's where we live,' he told her. 'My planet is just a few million miles away from it,' he added glibly.

In the stillness of the night, Tom went very quiet.

'What's the matter?' she whispered, noticing the pinpricks of starlight reflected in the large pupils of his tearful eyes.

Tom shrugged. 'I'm not really sure; I suppose I'm worried about Anya and her tiny calf in that cave. She must think by now that I have abandoned her—'

'I know Anya well,' said Winnie. 'She won't be thinking anything of the sort . . . I promise you.'

'Well, I also feel responsible for what happened to Berta. That avalanche was my idea. She had the chance to run away but came back to save me. It looks like that decision cost Berta her life,' he whispered gravely. 'I owe her my life so if there's any way of saving her, I need to find her. The truth is, I've grown so fond of your family, I'm not even sure I want to go home . . .' he paused, 'at least, not until I know what has . . .'

His faltering voice was drowned out by a sudden deep, wheezy snore, 'Szhcnuuuurrrrrggghhh!' Truba was sleeping peacefully.

Winnie pulled Tom closer to her warm body to comfort and protect him from the wailing wind. She felt him juddering as he burrowed into her dense woolly coat.

Was he shivering with cold or was he silently sobbing? She wasn't sure but she gently cuddled the young boy snuggling into her and poured her hot, misty breath over him.

Tom felt safe and secure in the embrace of this huge beast. He sank even deeper between the strands of her long matted hair. He lay there listening to the rhythmic drum beat of her heart, feeling his eyes growing heavy as tiredness began to overwhelm him. He drifted quietly off to sleep beneath the pepper-dust sky, vaguely aware of the large grey clouds sailing serenely overhead.

Soon, everyone was fast asleep.

LOOK WHO'S BACK

In the dead of night Winnie felt something prodding her. She stirred awake and peered into the semi-darkness. Was she dreaming? A small calf was sniffing and licking her fur. She opened her eyes even wider and beneath the vague moon could just make out the blurred face of Anya beaming proudly through the gloom.

'Hi Winnie, I've brought someone very special to meet you,' she whispered.

It took a few moments for Winnie's eyes to adjust

to the dimness. She leapt to her feet when she realised Anya had not returned alone from Crystal Cave. 'How did you find us here in the middle of the night?'

'Truba brought us here,' grinned Anya.

Winnie's face wrinkled with confusion. 'No, that's not possible!' she exclaimed. 'He has been with us all the time. Listen . . .' she paused as Truba's trembling trunk blew another rasping whistle.

'Szhcnuuuurrrrrggghhh . . .'

'See? He's still fast asleep!'

'Exactly!' giggled Anya. 'We heard him snoring from high up in the mountains, it was echoing everywhere. We followed the sound and that's how we knew where you were.'

Winnie rolled her large head from side to side. 'Typical!' she exclaimed. She playfully kicked Truba who gave out a loud grunt and blearily opened his eyes.

'I heard the avalanche rumbling too,' said Anya.

'Is everyone okay?'

Winnie shook her head sadly. 'No, I'm afraid not. We lost Berta.'

'Lost her? You mean . . . she's dead?'

'We don't know for sure, we can't find her but we think she is buried somewhere under the avalanche. So much snow, so much snow,' she repeated sorrowfully. 'We're going to carry on searching at first light.'

Winnie called over to Troyka who was still dozing nearby.

'Hey Troyka, come here. Look who has come back to us!' The giant mammoth clambered groggily to his feet.

'How did you manage to move the big boulder all by yourself?' he yawned.

'Well I wasn't exactly on my own,' grinned Anya. 'Your new daughter helped me push it away!'

Troyka squinted at a small black silhouette standing by Anya's side. He stepped forward, laid his trunk carefully over her, and gave the youngster a joyous hug.

The mammoths gathered round the new member of the herd.

Anya turned to Truba. 'I hear we've lost Berta.'

Truba nodded. 'It feels like we've searched everywhere,' he explained. 'But...' he shook his head with sadness. 'But it's like finding a, erm ...' his voice trailed off as he stared tearfully at the ground.

'A needle in a haystack?' suggested Tom helpfully.

Anya shot him a puzzled look. 'A what?'

'A needle in a haystack,' he repeated. 'It's an expression we use back home when something is difficult to find.'

'What's a needle?' asked Anya.

'What's a haystack?' added Truba.

Tom shook his head. 'It's not important,' he said softly. 'What matters right now is finding Berta.'

'We must carry on searching,' Anya told them.

'You are right Anya, but there's no way we'll ever find her in the middle of the night,' explained Winnie. 'We'll start looking again as soon as it gets lighter.'

'You promise?' pleaded Anya.

'We promise!' replied Troyka firmly.

'What about the wolves?' she asked. 'If any of them survived the avalanche, they may be out there waiting and watching. Even if they can't see us in the dark, they will surely smell us.'

Truba shook his head firmly. 'No,' he said. 'We've already found several wolves that didn't make it. I think the others are buried under the snow too.'

Troyka nodded. 'There has been no sign of them since the avalanche,' he said. 'We're fairly sure they all perished.'

Anya suddenly had a thought. 'Hey, why wait till morning?' she shrieked. 'You could use Little Bear's moonstick to guide you. It will help you to see where you're digging.'

'Moonstick?' they chorused. 'What's one of those?'

Anya turned to Tom. 'Tell them about your magic moonstick,' she urged him. 'Show them what it can do.'

Tom explained how his torch borrowed some of the light from the moon before giving it back whenever the moon went away or when it was hiding behind the clouds. Unconvinced, the mammoths began muttering. He told them how it shone even in the darkest night.

Anya nodded. 'He's right, I even saw it shining inside Crystal Cave, it was quite magical. Show them, Tom, let them see for themselves.'

'Okay,' he said as he delved into his backpack. 'With my moonstick, we will be able to carry on searching for poor Berta, and if she is under the snow, we need to get her out as quickly as possible.'

Tom groped inside his bag but apart from Katie's scarf there was nothing in it, not even the goggles he would need to get home. He patted the pockets of his coat – they were empty. He remembered he had looped the strap over his wrist, then recalled feeling a sickening pain when the avalanche had torn him from Berta as she had struggled to save him.

He peeled back his sleeve to reveal a big purple bruise where the strap had been wrenched away. That must have been the moment the moonstick was lost.

A BEAM OF HOPE

Dreaded thoughts crept across Tom's mind; he realised there was now no way of getting back to his family. Without the headset, he was stranded on this cold, bleak, lonely planet with no possible way of escape. Staring into the darkness he also knew there was no chance of ever finding it under all that snow.

'Don't worry, Tom, somehow we will help you to find your moonstick,' said Anya soothingly.

Even though it was quite dark, Tom turned his head towards the ice-strewn slopes.

'I don't think we'll ever find it under all that!' he told them softly, his lips trembling as he spoke. He thought of the snow that had oozed as creamy lava which now lay like a cloak draped over the side of Crystal Mountain.

After comforting Tom for several minutes, the mammoths began the seemingly hopeless task of trying to find Berta. As they carefully probed, prodded, and poked their tusks into the icy ground, dark clouds rumbled over the glacier. Strung out like a black hammock between the mountains, they brought flecks of fresh snow blotting out what remained of the pale moonlight.

Total darkness had now settled into the valley. Well almost total darkness, Anya saw it first: a faint glow, close to a clump of snapped trees where the avalanche had first ploughed into the herd.

'Look, it's a moonbeam!' she cooed. 'Maybe it's a

sign; as if it's trying to guide us to Berta.'

'Can't be,' replied Troyka wearily. 'Look above you Anya – there is no moon!'

He was right, not a single light pierced the cloud-laden sky.

'Maybe not, but it's a moonbeam alright,' she insisted. Anya bounded over to the luminous patch and dug her tusks under the snow. Within seconds she held something aloft with the tip of her trunk. 'See!' she screamed gleefully. 'I told you it was a moonbeam.' She had found the precious moonstick.

Tom Lennox had a sudden thought. 'Hey, Berta was beside me when the avalanche hit us, I'm sure that was when I lost this!' He noticed that the thin wrist strap was broken.

'Why are you so bothered about your moonstick?' yelled Truba. 'Don't you think you should be more concerned about Berta buried somewhere beneath us?'

Winnie leant forward. 'Yes, but don't you see? If he is right, Berta might be very close by.'

And so, as if their energies had been rekindled by fresh light blazing from the moonstick, the mammoths began to dig by swishing their tusks from side to side like giant scythes. Tom lit the way as the herd swiped away the snow.

Anya smiled proudly as she noticed her young calf joining in. Although she had no tusks yet, the youngster pawed away the snow and sniffed at the ground with her tiny trunk.

It wasn't long before Winnie prodded something soft about a metre below the surface. 'Quick!' she cried out. 'Shine the light over here.' Everyone gathered round as Winnie carefully pushed aside a broken tree to reveal a thick tuft of brown hair. She gently scraped away the remaining snow and moments later, they were gazing down sorrowfully at Berta's lifeless body.

Troyka sobbed silently as he tenderly slid his thick tusks under Berta. He lovingly raised her out of the snow hole before spreading her floppy, lifeless body before the mournful mammoths.

AT A PINCH

'She's not breathing,' wailed Truba.

They stood round staring helplessly. Anya's calf, sensing the mammoths' sadness, snuggled into her mother's coarse hair.

Tom felt sad. He squatted in the snow wondering if there was anything he could do for Berta. After all, she had saved his life up on the mountain when she'd protected him from the full force of the avalanche.

A memory suddenly popped into his head; he could clearly see his teacher, Mrs Newton, showing the class how people who stop breathing can sometimes be brought back to life. Tom began to wonder if the same could be done to a fully grown mammoth.

He jumped to his feet. 'Quick!' he screamed. 'I think I know how we can still help Berta.'

'How can we possibly help her now?' Winnie asked.

'We need to massage her chest', he told them. 'Whilst Tr—'

'Massage her chest?' screamed Truba scornfully. 'What good is that going to do?'

'Yes, massage her chest,' repeated Tom calmly. 'While one of us . . . one of you,' he corrected himself, 'blows into her mouth.'

'Blows into her mouth?' questioned Truba mockingly. 'And what is that supposed to do? Bring her back to life?'

'Yes Truba yes!' retorted Tom. 'That's exactly

what it's supposed to do!'

This was a step too far for the mammoths. They gaped open-mouthed at Tom – had he gone crazy?

Winnie was the first to break their silence. 'First you tell us to move that mountain!' she bawled angrily. 'And now you expect us to revive poor Berta as if she had simply fallen asleep!'

Tom could see the mammoths were all turning against him. 'Well my last idea worked; didn't the avalanche save us from being eaten by wolves?'

'Well . . . yes it did, but look at Berta,' Truba gestured at the stricken mammoth. 'Your avalanche didn't save her, did it?'

Tom Lennox stared guiltily at the ground, 'Yes but—'

'Yes but nothing!' interrupted Truba rudely. 'Poor Berta is lying there because of you, and that's all there is to it.'

'I'm so sorry,' said Tom earnestly. 'But please trust me. This plan might not work at all, but surely we should give it a try. We need to hurry because if we don't do it straight away, it'll definitely be too late to save her.'

'Okay, what do we have to lose? We'll do it!' said Troyka decisively.

Tom dropped to his knees quickly forcing his hand into Berta's mouth to clear away a chunk of ice. 'Great,' he said. 'We need to start by pummelling her chest.' He made a pushing motion with his hands to show the mammoths what he meant.

There was a scuffle as Truba fell to his knees.

'Nooooo, not you Truba, you might crush her completely! In any case we will need your big trunk to cover her mouth.'

Truba spread the end of his trunk over Berta's mouth and gently blew while Anya pumped and pounded on her chest.

Several tense minutes passed. Nothing happened. Anya looked at Tom for guidance. 'Shall we stop? It doesn't seem to be working.'

'No, please keep going.'

Once again, she noticed him putting the tips of his fingers to his lips in deep thought. She had seen him do the same when they were trapped in Crystal Cave. He had come up with a solution then – would he think of something now to save Berta's life?

Tom watched the two mammoths working hard to revive Berta. He realised something they were doing was wrong – or perhaps it was something they weren't doing at all? What was it?

He remembered how his teacher had used a dummy to demonstrate artificial respiration. He could see her clearly in his mind's eye: she was pressing down on its chest, just like Anya was now doing to Berta, then she was blowing into its mouth – Truba was doing that too. But Mrs Newton had been doing something else – what on earth was it?

He pictured his teacher working on the dummy, fumbling with its face, forgetting to do something vital – what was it? What had she overlooked?

The children had sniggered when Mrs Newton's cheeks turned purple as she blew fruitlessly into its mouth.

But the class eventually clapped and cheered when she finally got it right and the dummy's chest began to rise and fall as if it was actually breathing.

The image was now so clear. Quick, think! Tom, think! What had she been forgetting to do?

Then it came to him – while she'd been pumping its chest and blowing into its mouth, Mrs Newton should have been squeezing the dummy's nose between her finger and thumb!

STEP ON IT

'I know what's wrong!' he shouted. 'Truba's breath isn't getting into her lungs. Troyka, you'll have to press on her trunk with your foot!'

'No chance! I'm not stamping on poor Berta,' Troyka replied defiantly.

'Wait Troyka, maybe Tom's right!' said Anya excitedly. 'Truba is breathing into her mouth and it's coming straight back out through her trunk. Look!'

Anya's explanation seemed to convince Troyka, so he stepped gently onto Berta's trunk to flatten it and once again Truba pumped his breath into her. This time her chest began to rise and fall.

They continued working on Berta's still body until eventually, she began to cough and splutter.

'Okay!' shouted Tom. 'Everyone stand back and give her some room.'

They watched anxiously as Berta lay on top of the snow gasping for breath. Several tense minutes passed before she opened her eyes and smiled. Tom's plan had worked. He had brought Berta back to life. The mammoths were overjoyed.

Berta's life had hung in the balance for many anxious moments, yet when the tension finally subsided, Truba spotted something new about the stricken mammoth's face. 'Look, part of her tusk has snapped off!'

Troyka gasped as Berta's trunk nursed the broken end of her tusk. 'Wow, she looks exactly like you again Winnie.'

Tom stared at Berta then glanced over at her twin before he began to laugh. 'Oh dear, it looks like you are back to square one!'

'What is square one? What do you mean?' asked Anya.

'Well, can you tell them apart? I know I can't.'

Shaking their heads Truba, Anya and Troyka gawped at the sisters; Tom was right: Winnie and Berta were identical twins once more.

Troyka turned to the little boy who had helped to save Anya and her calf from the hungry wolves, brought a mountain to its knees, and miraculously brought Berta back from the dead. 'We can never thank you enough for all you've done. If it weren't for you, the wolves would have killed one of us,' he said tearfully. 'Anya would have had to leave the cave eventually and both she and our little calf would have been at their mercy.'

Tom looked bashful as he held up his moonstick. 'I think you really need to thank this,' he replied with a grin. 'If it weren't for this I wouldn't have escaped from Crystal Cave to warn you, but I admit I was terrified when the wolves cornered me on the mountain. I even thought about putting on my special goggles and going home!' he told the mammoths shamefully.

'Aha, but you didn't, did you?' said Winnie, proudly coiling her thick trunk around Tom's waist and squeezing him affectionately – perhaps even a little too tightly! 'Anyway, what are goggles, and how do they make you disappear? Can you show us?'

'I only wish I could,' he whimpered. 'But I think I must have lost them in the avalanche, they'll be somewhere under all that snow. Without my goggles I have no way of returning home, so it looks like you are going to be my new family from now on.' Tears formed tiny ice globes on his cheeks as he gently sobbed.

There was a brief commotion as the small calf passed something to her mother.

'Erm, do you mean these Little Bear?' Anya stepped forward with Tom's goggles perched comically on the end of her trunk.

A large smile spread across his face. 'Thank you. Where were they?'

'I didn't find them . . . she did!' Anya nodded towards her calf. 'They must have fallen out of your bag; she spotted them glinting on the floor of the cave as we were leaving. You must have dropped them there.' She gently shunted the youngster towards Tom who held out his arms to give the little mammoth a huge hug.

FUNNY OLD GAME

Cold, grey dawn was slowly peeling away the dark night as heavy snow began to fall once again, the creamy flakes fluttering in the air like frantic moths.

Tom shivered; he hated the idea of leaving the mammoths, but oh, how he longed to get back to his warm cosy bed. His soaking wet foot was now throbbing steadily with pain from the intense cold. 'I think I had better go home,' he announced sadly.

Troyka stepped towards him. 'We'd love you to

stay and be part of our family,' he said affectionately.

'I'm sorry Troyka I can't. Even though I have grown so fond of you all, I would love to spend more time here, but I need to get back to my own world before my family starts to miss me. They don't even know where I am. Come to think of it, I'm not even sure that I do!' They all started giggling.

'Besides which,' continued Tom. 'I'm playing football tomorrow, so I ought to be heading home—'

'Football? What's football?' asked Berta.

Tom instantly regretted mentioning the word; this was going to take a lot of explaining! 'Well,' he began. 'A football is erm, well, it's a bag shaped a bit like a full moon which is filled with air. It's about this size,' he held his hands apart, 'then we kick it to each other with our feet which is why it's called foo—'

'Yeah, we get it – football,' said Truba.

Tom could see the mammoths growing very

perplexed. The problem was, the more he thought about the game of football, the more ridiculous it sounded – even to him.

'Well if you ask me, I think it sounds rather stupid!' sniggered Berta. Her family all nodded.

'I suppose it does when you really think about it,' agreed Tom, and they all began to laugh.

Troyka was soon wearing a more serious expression. He was puzzling over what Tom had said earlier about him being a space voyager.

Anya could tell what was on his mind; she tapped Troyka playfully with her trunk. 'It's simple really, you see our Little Bear is a time adventurer.' She pointed her trunk up to the sky. 'He comes from somewhere out there, far beyond our stars. A place we can never go to ... isn't that right?' she winked at Tom.

'Actually, I think you'll find he comes from over

there!' said Winnie smugly. She hoisted her own trunk and pointed it in the opposite direction to Anya's. 'He lives in the Wilky May – or something like that.'

Tom smiled at Winnie's pronunciation but nodded. 'You're both right – kind of. Although I must correct you on one thing Anya, like I've been telling you, I'm not a bear at all, I'm a boy!' he shrilled.

'Yeah, but to us you're just a lovely, little brave bear, and that's how we will always remember you.' She smiled tenderly.

Troyka shrugged. 'Well I have no idea where you are going, or how you plan to get there,' he said. 'But before you set off we all want to thank you for saving our lives from the wolves.'

'What do you mean?' exclaimed Truba, 'It was me who brought the snow down from Crystal Mountain, with this!' He extended his long trunk and blew a loud snort, causing the snowflakes to dance and swirl.

'PHHHHEEEEUUUURR—'

'Woah Truba!' screamed Berta. 'Pipe down, or you'll set off another avalanche with your silly, big trunk. I've eaten quite enough snow for one day thank you!'

She gave Tom a playful nudge to let him know she had glimpsed the lick of lightning and heard the thunder that had really shaken the mountain. 'We'll let Truba believe he did it all on his own ... otherwise he'll sulk for days,' she whispered.

PARTING OF THE WAYS

'Well, I'll be off then,' said Tom.

He was just pulling on his headset when Anya stopped him. 'I need to tell you something before you go,' she said. 'While you were fighting wolves and helping Truba to demolish mountains, I sat down in Crystal Cave and eventually, I came up with a name for my baby; something that will always remind us of you. I'm calling her . . . Mishka.'

'Mishka? That's a lovely name,' replied Tom. 'But why should it make you think of me?'

'It's because here in Siberia, Mishka means Little Bear!' she chuckled.

'But I keep telling you, I'm not—'

'We know,' the mammoths all chorused. 'You're not a bear, you're a boy!' They laughed raucously.

As he said goodbye, Tom fondly patted each of the mammoths, then he wrapped his arms around Anya's trunk and gave her a huge hug.

'Do you promise to come back and see us again soon Little Bear?' she asked. 'We're going to miss you.'

'I will try Anya, I promise you I will try.'

As he was about to leave, he handed the moonstick to Mishka. 'I want you to have this,' he told her softly. 'It gets very dark around here, so I think you need it more than I do. Press this button to switch it on and off, I don't suppose it will last forever but for now it will guide you on your path between the mountains.'

He reached for his headset. The mammoths gasped in amazement as he slipped it on and slowly dissolved among the snowflakes before their disbelieving eyes.

Mishka stared open-mouthed. 'Wow! Did you see that mum? How is that even possible?'

Anya shrugged. 'Who knows?' she replied softly.

'How did he just vanish into thin air like that?' asked Truba, screwing up his eyes against the strengthening snowfall.

'I'm not sure,' murmured Anya tearfully. 'But I am certain he will be back one day.' Then she turned away. 'Come on,' she said. 'Let's go find something to eat and a place to shelter.'

Knowing there were no more wolves to terrorise them, the family set off on a solemn trek up through the mountains in search of fresh food. Mishka proudly held aloft her magic moonstick, ready to light their way when night time returned.

RETURN JOURNEY

Tom quickly retraced his flight path through a maze of galaxies. He carefully threaded his way among the stars and moments later, was back in his bedroom. Tired, cold, and desperate for sleep, he put his headset back in its box and closed his bedside drawer. But he still had one more task to complete before climbing into bed.

Quietly, so as not to wake his sleeping sister, he sneaked into her room and pushed the battered wet winter clothes to the back of her wardrobe. Katie's lovely scarf had become a long, gnarled, tattered rag. Her once beautiful jumper was now dirty and unwearable – Tom noticed that the mammoth on the front was looking sadder than ever. Her cream duffel coat was smudged with dirt and had been ripped on the shoulder by the wolf's fangs. He glanced at Katie's favourite winter boots permanently ruined by the Siberian lake's brackish water. Ah, but would she notice all this damage to her clothes? Too right she would!

Returning to his own bedroom, he slid under the duvet and closed his eyes. Tomorrow he would get up early and write notes in his diary about his fantastic Arctic adventure. The last thing he heard before drifting off to sleep was the hooting of a lonely owl.

'Wooit wooit toohooo'

BORN SURVIVOR

L ater that day, 33,000 years ago.

The snow had finally stopped falling. A hungry snowy owl sat in silence watching shadows cast from the mountain stealing across the Siberian wilderness. As it perched patiently in a lone pine tree on the border of the devastated forest, a swift movement caught its attentive eyes.

The owl quietly flexed its bristling wing feathers as a white Arctic hare scurried over the blocks of snow churned by the avalanche. The hare paused to scratch itself. The owl poised to swoop.

Then, out of the dark silence came an unfamiliar sound,

Scritsscchh, scritsscchh, - scritsscchh, scritsscchh, - scritsscchh, scritsscchh.

The hare stiffened, sensing danger, its eyes and ears fully alert. The owl had heard it too. Together they listened and watched. The hare tensed her legs, ready to scamper away. The owl spread his wings ready to scoop up the hare and carry it off to the nest where impatient chicks were waiting to be fed.

The noise grew stronger:

scritsscchh, scritsscchh, scritsscchh.

Something trapped beneath the snowy rubble was beginning to burrow its way out.

Slowly, doggedly, she twisted her body until she was able to stretch out and start clawing at the soft snow that entombed her. Inch by painful inch she scraped and scratched until she had carved a slender tunnel to freedom.

The startled hare felt a tremor in her tiny paws as the snow shifted beneath her. She hesitated momentarily, then she was off, fleeing as fast as the Arctic wind; too quick for the wide-eyed owl who held his position on the branch, hoping that the scraping sound was a plump rodent burrowing out of the ground.

All of a sudden two large paws burst from the snow, quickly followed by a twitching black nose gulping in the fresh air.

Shortly afterwards, a bedraggled lone wolf hauled herself groggily from her wintry grave. She clambered out onto the frosty surface, stretched and began to shake the loose snow from her fur. It was Nadiya.

Squinting through narrowed eyes to dim the glinting sunlight, she gazed across the glacier. The snowfall had destroyed everything. The forest was gone apart from a few splintered trees poking out of the ground. She watched the disappointed owl flap gracefully away.

What about her wolf family? Had they been destroyed too? She guessed they were all deep under the collapsed mountain – buried forever. She faced west in the direction of Crystal Cave. At least her beloved Prince was still somewhere up over that ridge – or so she thought. She hoped he had found the hidden tunnel into the cave.

Right now Nadiya was all alone. Well almost alone; she began to feel her restless pups squirming inside her, they were getting ready to be born.

Nadiya knew she could not give birth on the frozen glacier. She decided to make her way to Crystal Cave where her puppies would be safe and warm. But what if that large stone was still sealing the mouth of the cave? She made up her mind to look for the secret passageway where she hoped Prince would be waiting.

After being buffeted and buried for so long, her legs ached with every step. Onwards she trudged, her path up into the mountains illuminated by the permafrost glittering under the moonlight. She stumbled upon the trail left earlier by the mammoths. 'So, at least they managed to survive!' she mumbled bitterly.

Finally reaching the crest of the ridge where the wolf pack had come so close to catching the strange man-child, her sharp eyes picked up the trail of paw prints left behind by Prince.

Standing perfectly still, sniffing the air, her keen nose picked up a sweet, tangy scent that was so familiar. She could taste it in the wind. Blood!

Instantly sensing danger, Nadiya drew back her lips bearing her sharp fangs, the coarse hairs on her back bristling. She crouched low, twisting her ears to listen for any hostile sounds. None!

Up ahead, she spotted a hole surrounded by freshly turned snow. She had found the secret entrance. She hunkered down low and cautiously crawled towards it, dragging her swollen tummy over the frozen surface.

She realised that something – or someone – had recently been pulled out from the cave hole and dragged over the linen-white land. The signs were unmistakeable.

As she got closer she spotted a long crimson smear leading up into the mountain. Alongside it were the telltale clawless paw marks of a large cat. She knew those footprints well, they belonged to her old enemy – Saiba.

Nadiya followed the dotted red trail for several metres brushing her nose lightly over the snow while she sniffed. Then all of a sudden, with her shoulders hunched in sorrow, she paused as she recognised the smell. She knew it very well indeed – it was Prince's scent.

Nadiya tilted her head and let out a long, mournful howl,

'Hoooouuuwwwwruuuuuuuuuuuuuuuuuuuuuuu!!'

Once again the lone wolf felt the pups inside her tummy rolling, turning, squirming. She retraced her steps and urgently squeezed her swollen body through the narrow cave entrance and disappeared into a maze of tunnels, hoping that no further danger lurked inside.

High above from the rocky platform outside

her lair, Saiba had heard Nadiya's anguished cry of sadness. She watched the wolf's tail vanish into the ground. Licking her blood-red lips she turned to her cubs. 'There'll be even more food tomorrow!' she promised with a sneer.

DOCTOR, DOCTOR

The next day – 33,000 years later.

'So what do you think it is doctor?' Tom's father watched closely as Doctor Millar gently inspected his son's discoloured toes.

After several moments, the doctor stood up scratching the dark stubble on his chin. Then he looked quizzically at the youngster. 'Hmmm. You're sure you haven't dropped anything on your foot Tom?'

'No.'

'Well have you stubbed your toes or tripped over something? Was that how you got that small nick above your eye?'

Tom Lennox shook his head firmly. 'No, definitely not.'

The doctor seemed lost in thought. 'Hmmm, strange, very strange indeed,' he muttered. 'Okay, so please tell me honestly how you think your foot came to look like this.'

Tom sighed, 'I've already told my dad, but he doesn't believe me, so why should you?'

'Try me,' said Doctor Millar earnestly.

Tom's father nodded. 'Go on son, tell the doctor. It'll help him to understand how your toes turned blue.'

Tom began his story. 'Well, I almost fell into a frozen lake . . .' He briefly described his adventure up to the moment the boot slipped off. Dr Millar's eyes grew wider and wider as Tom's tale became more and more fanciful. ' . . . But I couldn't get to it because the water was too cold and too deep,' he continued, 'so Truba pulled Katie's boot out of the water for me. Eventually my foot got so cold, I had to come home.'

'And Katie is . . . ?'

'She's my sister.'

'Oh, so she was there too?'

'No, I went alone but I needed to borrow some of her warm winter clothes including her boots.'

Doctor Millar was becoming very confused. He turned to Tom's father. 'So who is Truba? Is that the nickname of one of his school friends?'

But it was Tom who answered the doctor's question by rolling his eyes before exclaiming, 'No of course not, Truba is a mammoth!' He said this as if it were the most obvious thing in the world. 'He's called Truba because of the shape of his trunk . . . it looks like a trumpet you see. We became friends when—'

Tom's father threw up his arms. 'Oh, I'm afraid he lives in a fantasy world doctor, he's always chasing after dinosaurs. Now he wants us to believe that he almost fell into a prehistoric icy lake.'

'I'm not making it up dad, really I'm not! In any case, Truba wasn't a dinosaur, he was a mammoth. You've read my adventure, you already know what happened.'

'Oh that's right doctor, this morning he was up at the crack of dawn scribbling about his erm – adventures.' Tom's father drew invisible speech marks in the air with his fingers before turning to his son. 'Why don't you show Doctor Millar your diary?'

Tom reached into his battered backpack and sheepishly handed it over.

Doctor Millar flicked through the pages and several minutes later re-examined the boy's toes with a magnifying glass.

'Unbelievable! Incredible!' he muttered loudly. 'Do you mind if I ask the doctor in the next surgery to take a look at your son's foot? I'd like a second opinion.'

Without waiting for an answer, he left the room clutching Tom's diary. He returned several minutes later with a friendly-looking woman who sported a thick mop of greying hair. She wore an unfastened white medical coat which gaped open.

As she strode into the room, Tom noticed a thick cream-coloured jumper underneath her gown. He could clearly see the motif on the front of it, and from the sideways smirk she gave him, he realised he was meant to. It was a smiling woolly mammoth adorned by flecks of snow – identical to the one he had worn on his travels!

Tom's mouth fell open with surprise, but before he could speak, she pressed a long elegant finger to her lips and quietly made a shushing motion.

Dr Millar pointed to a chair and invited her to sit down.

'This is my colleague Dr Shakim,' he announced. 'I have asked her to take a quick look at your son's toes. I've told her what I think it might be.' Then with a disbelieving sneer, he added, 'I have also asked her to read Tom's amazing story about the Siberian mammoths.'

Dr Shakim perched on the edge of a chair, balanced a pair of small round spectacles on the tip of her upturned nose and was soon busily flicking through the pages of Tom's journal.

'Hmmm, you've obviously had quite an adventure young man,' she said with a wry smile. 'I know how cold it can be in Siberia. By the way, I read in your personal log that you also got a nasty bruise on your wrist. May I take a peek?'

Dr Shakim took hold of Tom's hand then closed her fist tightly around the injured area. Tom felt a warm sensation creeping up his arm. After several seconds, she let go, and by the time Tom managed to pull back his sleeve, the bruise which had been so vivid, had completely vanished!

Tom gasped in amazement.

Removing her reading glasses from the end of her nose, Dr Shakim bent to take a closer look at the foot and slowly began to massage the purple skin. Once again he felt warmth oozing from her touch.

While she was stooping low, Tom noticed her name badge dangling from a lanyard looped around her neck.

For some reason he found himself rearranging the letters of her name in his head. 'That's really weird,' he mumbled.

'What's weird Tom?' asked Dr Millar.

'Oh nothing really, it's just that "Shakim" is an anagram of Mish—'

Dr Shakim instantly sprang up and stopped Tom from finishing what he was about to say. 'Okay Tom, that's fine, you can put your shoe and sock back on now.' She handed the journal back to him as he eyed her suspiciously.

'Well,' she sighed. 'You know what I think?' she looked at their expectant faces. 'I believe your son might just be telling us the truth, because he really is suffering from mild frostbite!' But there's nothing to worry about, it will clear up almost straight away.'

'Frostbite?' queried Tom's father. 'That's impossible, we haven't even had any rain for four weeks never mind snow. It's the middle of summer, doctor. Look at the weather outside!'

They all turned and gazed out of the window where swifts and swallows swooped energetically beneath the blazing sun in a cloudless August sky.

'Your father has a point Tom,' said Dr Millar. 'We haven't seen snow or ice for many months. So tell me, when did this happen to your foot?'

'Oh it was about 33,000 years ago,' Tom replied

with a grin. 'But it seems like only yesterday!'

As he hobbled out of the surgery, Tom felt the pain already starting to ebb away from his frostbitten toes where Dr Shakim had touched his foot. He turned to look back at her. 'Oh, by the way doctor . . . ' She looked up from the medical notes she was reading. 'Did you know that if you rearrange the letters of your name, it spells—'

'Yes I did!' Once again, she had interrupted him before he could finish what he was trying to say. Then with an exaggerated wink of her eye, she added, 'And isn't that a very strange coincidence indeed?'

Tom stuffed the diary into his backpack which flipped over when the shoulder strap slipped through his fingers. Something clattered loudly onto the wooden floor.

Dr Millar picked up the object and held it to the light. It was an oval chunk of crystal, slightly larger than a hen's egg, that fitted snugly into the palm of his hand. One of its edges had been sharpened into a crude blade that had become worn and scratched . . .

ACKNOWLEDGEMENTS

Special thanks to three very talented people who helped turn my story into a turn of the page: Agatha Smith a wonderful creative who designed the cover and the book layout, Charlie Taylor who brought my characters to life through her extraordinary illustrations and Gemma Eno for her fantastic, forensic proofreading skills.

Grateful thanks to my great friend Don Millar who, regrettably, is no longer with us, but who made this implausible story entirely possible!

ABOUT THE AUTHOR

Although his family roots are firmly embedded in the northeast of England, Simon E Wilkinson has lived in Yorkshire most of his life.

A former government press officer, newspaper theatre critic and radio broadcaster, he has edited several non-fiction books and articles.

Simon continues to write for local journals and now devotes much of his time to writing children's fiction. More books in the Tom Lennox series are scheduled for publication.

Quirky fact: during his early teens, with only Penny the cocker spaniel, a noisy tawny owl and the occasional fox for company, Simon slept in his parent's garden shed for three long, cold years! Underneath that shed lived a large grey rat . . .

Printed in Great Britain
by Amazon

32797769R00131